The Scorpion of Empendwe

The Scorpion of Empendwe

William Turnbull

Writer's Showcase
presented by *Writer's Digest*
San Jose New York Lincoln Shanghai

The Scorpion of Empendwe

Writer's Showcase
presented by *Writer's Digest*
an imprint of iUniverse.com, Inc.

For information address:
iUniverse.com, Inc.
620 North 48th Street
Suite 201
Lincoln, NE 68504-3467
www.iuniverse.com

ISBN: 0-595-12634-0

Printed in the United States of America

A story of action and suspense

A deserted mine in the heart of Africa, a dark secret hidden in its depths...a Russian mafioso, from his chateau in the Cayman Islands, engineering a horrific catastrophe at the mine with the help of a corrupt insurance executive...the story runs the gamut of international intrigue, romance and passion, suspense, horror and revenge.

"Grittily authentic...had me turning the pages...the action scenes are prima...the African scenes are written with a rare feel for the beauty of the place...this is very good stuff indeed...there's movie potential here."

—Novelist Chris Scott

I

The deserted mine at Empendwe lay at the bottom of a funnel-shaped crater that reminded Wim Van Dyk of an ant-lion's sand pit. A stone kicked over the edge set off a thirty-foot landslide. He swore.

Van Dyk and three other men had reached Empendwe after jolting three hundred miles through the Zambian bush in a convoy of pickups, trailers and a seven-ton truck. They were there to reopen the mine.

After ten hours in temperatures of a hundred and twenty-eight degrees, the first priority was beer, and the nearest source of it was a Lozi village of thatched mud huts about a mile away. Two of the men made the trip in one of the pickups, returning half an hour later with crates of Castle lager. They also brought a man they had hired as cook.

Van Dyk hooked two bottles together by the caps, wrenched one open and swigged long and hard at the hot brew. He calculated that to collar the shaft would take at least three thousand tons of concrete. The work of pumping out, re-equipping and extending the mine would follow.

The hired man cooked a pot of sema and barbecued half a dozen pheasants they had shot on the way. They ate as darkness fell, throwing the bones into the fire, their faces bathed in its glow. From the darkness beyond, they could hear the sounds of the village—dogs barking, fowl squawking, shrill cries of children, a man talking. The sounds floated close by on the sultry night air, as though the village were only yards away. Even closer at hand, a nightjar screeched, mosquitoes whined, a bat fluttered.

Resting on his elbow, Van Dyk tilted his head back and gazed up at the gossamer threads of the Milky Way. Surrounded by pitch-darkness, beneath the infinite expanse of the galaxy, so crystal-clear in the tropical night sky, he was overwhelmed by a sense of eternity, a sense of freedom.

He reached for another beer. "The gear can wait," he said, more or less to himself.

There was no argument. The men were too relaxed to think of unpacking the trailers that night.

They fell asleep beside the embers of the fire, confident in themselves and their future, at one with their surroundings.

*   *   *

On the same late September evening, a man sat nursing a drink on the patio of his lakefront home in Toronto, Canada. Two miles away lay the city, its lights shimmering through the trees on his right. Directly ahead, the lake was in darkness, a fathomless void. Only the gentle lapping of the waves, and the occasional rustling of the branches, broke the silence.

He shivered slightly in the quickening breeze and was throwing back the rest of his scotch when a telephone buzzed on the patio table beside him. He put the instrument to his ear, switching it on as he did so.

"Chamberlain?" The voice at the other end, deep and slightly hollow, sounded Eastern European, perhaps Russian.

"Anton! I've been waiting for your call. Starting to get a bit chilly outside." Chamberlain spoke with an Irish accent, and with a boyish eagerness at odds with his grey hair.

"Are you ready to proceed?" the voice continued as if Chamberlain had not spoken.

"Well, there are some details to be worked out. The reinsurance…"

"The mine will be operating by May."

"Yes."

"By then I need thirty million, and by September, a hundred million coverage."

"When will the…" Chamberlain's voice tailed off.

"What will happen, I make the arrangements. You are paid when we are paid."

"We'll have to go over the details. The inventory, the projected sales, the application…"

"I am here on Cayman Islands until three weeks from now."

"That doesn't give me much time. I have to be in Montreal next…"

"I am sure for ten million of your dollars you are going to find a way…I wait for your call."

Chamberlain slowly took the telephone from his ear and rested it on the table. He stared into the darkness in front of him, trying to collect his thoughts.

The stakes were much higher this time. Ten million dollars made him salivate, but at the same time he felt a stab of fear. He imagined being caught, losing his prominent position with the company, having to sell his house, his cottage and his Mercedes to pay defence lawyers. He thought of the publicity, the shame his wife and daughter would have to live with. He saw himself as a living corpse in jail, trying to assume a nonchalant facade, trying to hide the leaden pain in his stomach.

With a wrenching effort, he rejected these images. He would arrange the insurance coverage, because Anton Turr had enough evidence to destroy him otherwise. At least the money would buy him a new identity, a change of venue, a clean break with the past.

He stood shakily, picked up the phone, the scotch and the empty glass and headed for the warm glow of his living room.

2

After a long, dry winter, September and October at Empendwe were unusually hot months that year. The grass had long since withered and disappeared, and the earth was crazed and furrowed with deep, wide cracks. When the crew showered in the cabins built during the first weeks at the mine, they had to wait almost until midnight until the water, poured into overhead drums during the day, had cooled to a bearable temperature. There was one consolation: in another climate they would have been drenched in sweat merely with the effort of lifting a beer, but here the sweat dried as fast as it flowed.

The day after their arrival, the men had hung chain ladders over the sides of the pit, securing them with stakes in the ground above. They had cleared debris from the perimeter of the shaft, laid wire matting around the sides of the funnel, and circled the rim of the shaft with an initial ten-foot-high sleeve of timber shuttering. As supplies were brought from Lusaka, forty miles away, local men were recruited to work on the minehead, mixing concrete and pouring it into the matrix to form a collar. They had used more than seventy thousand bags of cement before the collar was complete, four months later.

While work on the minehead proceeded, Van Dyk had additional quarters built for staff due to arrive in the New Year. The contractor enlarged the original cabins and equipped them with plumbing and electricity. A five-hundred-foot bore hole had provided an abundance of water, so a swimming pool was installed. On instructions from the owner, a runway was also built, and in November, when the first showers were beginning to fall, it was inaugurated by his arrival.

The man who climbed out of the twin-engined Cessna towered over Van Dyk, who was himself over six feet tall. As they shook hands, he looked hard at Wim without speaking.

"Mr.Turr. We finally meet. You found us without any difficulty." Wim spoke with the precise but courteous intonation of an Afrikaner.

"I know where to find you." Still there was no hint of a smile.

Wim drove him across the quarter mile separating the runway from the residential enclave, which Turr passed apparently without a glance, then up the track leading to the mine. "Thank you for your help—the line of credit especially," he told Turr. "When we first arrived we had no idea what to expect."

Turr grunted. He was wedged in the passenger seat of the pickup, half-facing Wim, with his right elbow jutting out of the window, his hand outside holding on to the roof. "I know what is needed," he said, watching Wim closely.

Wim felt the man's eyes on him, but did not find his voice unfriendly or patronizing. He seemed detached, but at the same time curious. Perhaps he was having difficulty relating to a young buck with long blond hair. Eventually he decided that Turr was there to check out the personnel he had hired through his agents in Johannesburg, to satisfy himself that they were as tough as the reports had indicated, and that they knew what they were doing.

They got out on the hillside near the minehead, at a point overlooking the slopes leading down to the Kafue Flats, and ultimately to the Kafue River, seven miles away. The grass was beginning to grow again, trees were in bud, and orabi, reedbuck and lechwe could be seen here and there in the distance. Turr stood for a moment, arrested by the view, then turned abruptly and headed for the mine.

At the work site, he spent less than a minute watching the crew mixing and pouring concrete, then headed down an incline on the other side. There was a plateau about five hundred yards away, slightly concave in the centre, overlooked by an adit in the hillside.

"This can be our tailings pond," Wim said as he followed Turr down the slope. "Probably this was where it was in the original mine."

Turr nodded, walked up to the adit, which had long since collapsed, then turned and ran his eyes slowly over the ground. When he eventually spoke, there was a gleam in his eye.

"I will send a geologist next month to work with you," he intoned. "I will also fax you instructions for the next stage of the mine development. Now, before I go, would you introduce me to your friends." The last sentence was not spoken as a question, but as a statement.

Wim shouted and waved at two men who were unloading lumber from one of the Toyota pickups near the work site. The men left their work and came over to meet him and Turr as they returned up the slope.

"Mr. Turr, meet Todd Delahaye and Stefan Kristiansson." The men shook hands with Turr, surprised at his size but not hesitating to return his direct gaze. "Sweeney" Delahaye, who like Wim Van Dyk had been an amateur boxer in his teens, had at one stage been national welterweight champion. Kristiansson, an engineer from Sweden who had been working in mines in the Copper Belt for two years, had been unknown to the others until the week before they set out for Empendwe.

"I think you have one more man," said Turr.

"Yes—Martin Porter...Martin!" He called out towards the work crew, and one of the men emerged, dusting concrete off his hands as he jogged over to meet Turr. He was a black man, of average height, solidly built and muscular. After shaking hands with Turr, he continued jogging on the spot, like a runner after a race.

"Martin's doing a stint on the collar," Wim told Turr. "We all take a turn every day. But for Martin, it's part of his workout." He and Martin were glad to have the excuse to laugh.

After questioning Martin for a few minutes about his experience in the mines in the Transvaal, Turr left. "I will see you in a few weeks...I will call you before I come out", he intoned as he got into the plane. Less than an hour after his arrival he was gone.

3

Across the quadrangle, a staircase wound upwards from a stone archway framing the commoners' garden and its ancient sycamore. A young woman climbed the wooden stairs, smoothed and hollowed by centuries of use. On the third landing, the outer door was open; she knocked on the inner door, waited a moment and took a discreet step inside.

There was a fragrance of pipe tobacco, a fire smouldering in the hearth. On either side of the fire were sagging armchairs in which student and tutor, once a week, would debate an arcane question of political theory. At the other end of the room, leaded casements, with faded red window seats, overlooked the Fellows' garden. It was a room to which generations of earnest young men had borne thin essays produced in the small hours, fortified in their exhaustion by thoughts of indolent hours to come; a room visited as earnestly on social occasions, until tart golden sherry had created a comfortable, loquacious blur.

A door on the right opened, and a figure stood in a dusty shaft of sunlight. The woman broke a frigid silence. "Professor Arnald...I came to see you," she said, fighting the man's rivetting gaze. "I need your help."

"Trying to remember which year you were," he murmured, his voice melodious and cultured, his rumpled appearance and unassuming shock of hair blending with the cultivated understatement of his surroundings. He motioned her to an upright chair.

"The year of Selya Paxton." She spoke lightly, goaded by the implication that she should identify herself by reference to someone else.

His back to the fire, Arnald began to fill his pipe, his comfortable stance, rather than his facial expression, betraying interest. Despite his feigned indifference, he had not forgotten Selya Paxton. One of the first "women" admitted to the college a few years ago, after five centuries, Selya had been the only student in his experience to have switched from politics to geology in midstream. But there was more to it than that.

Born and raised in Africa, Selya's father, Colonel Ben Paxton, had stayed on after independence as Chief of National Security and right-hand man to the President of Zambia. While researching Paxton's background for the British Foreign Office, Arnald had pieced together a story that had intrigued and haunted him ever since.

In 1879, Brigadier Cecil Paxton, Ben's great-great-grandfather, had led a battalion of Highlanders against the Zulus, and through an obsessive determination to accomplish his mission at any cost, had prevailed amid carnage. Among the surrendering chieftains, one had the audacity, as Paxton saw it, to offer him a woman. He had turned on his heel, then halted abruptly, confronted by the most arresting beauty he had ever seen.

Her arms held on either side by two tribesmen, she had looked at him with a clear-eyed but distant expression, almost as if she were not of the same time and place. Her complexion was pale, her eyes hazel, and his first thought was that she was a survivor of some doomed Boer expedition. He remembered that the first

Boers to enter Zulu territory, bibles in hand, had been massacred to a man forty years earlier. But something told him otherwise.

After the Zulu War, Brigadier Paxton had retired to England to live in relative obscurity with his strangely beautiful bride. Few people beyond the stone walls surrounding his country estate in Derbyshire knew her story, and apart from Paxton, no-one knew of her Huguenot ancestry, revealed by the chief and elders under questioning and by her own distant recollection of the French language, last heard as a girl of five before the slaughter of her community in a tribal massacre.

Selya had been under Arnold's tutelage when he was asked to look into her father's background. It had been helpful to be able to speak to her about her father, although he had been careful to give the impression that his main interest was the political development of the country, tinged with a friendly concern for Paxton's well-being. Whenever he looked into her eyes, however, he had the disconcerting feeling that he was looking into the eyes which had mesmerized the brigadier, so many years ago.

"You had something to say to me?" he said eventually through a haze of smoke, turning to throw a match into the fire, then turning back to gaze across the room and through the windows on the opposite side, at the ancient walls and slate rooftops across the quadrangle.

"Something seems to be happening in Zambia."

"You've spoken to your father?"

"He rang last night, in the middle of the night. He said very little—only that I shouldn't go back there just now."

"Nothing else?"

"I asked whether a coup was taking place—I didn't know what to say. He said no, something to do with his work."

"A security problem?"

"He wouldn't say anything else."

"I'll see what I can do. Where can I reach you?"

"In London." She wrote down the telephone number. "This is my work number—it's a firm of consulting engineers."

"Now I do have a few things to do."

As he ushered her out, she apologised for the intrusion, and their eyes met for a brief moment. He looked into their hazel beauty, so clear and yet so strangely distant, and winced.

4

After the rains came, in two or three weeks the grass was knee-deep, the trees were in leaf and the landscape had changed from brown to green. In another month, the grass would be at shoulder height, hard to see over from the cab of a pickup, and the wild life would multiply within its cover. Until June, when they became visible targets for game hunters after the grass had been burned off, the land would be teeming with reedbuck, daika, seti-tungu, and above all orabi.

In November, as the Kafue River rose, the land above it also teemed with scorpions seeking higher ground. That year, after the drought had concentrated them close to the river, they were unusually profuse and adventurous, finding their way to Empendwe, where they congregated in the damp, shady areas under the trailers and cabins. They also found their way under the teak floor grids in the shower stalls, which the men would remove as part of their nightly ritual, uncovering and killing them before taking their shower.

The more civilized quarters now enjoyed by Van Dyk and his colleagues not only spared them the hazard of finding scorpions in the shower, but also provided appropriate accommodation for female guests, usually nurses from Lusaka. The girls came out with the men at weekends, on the face of it to attend a party, but perfectly aware of the unspoken reality that once there they had a choice: stay the night or walk back forty miles through the bush.

Such a party took place on the Saturday before the geologist was due to arrive, at the beginning of December. Along with the harvest of nurses, Wim had invited a mining equipment representative, a hardware salesman from GKN and two prospective foremen, at the mine on business that day, to stay for the evening.

The party was held in a building at one end of the swimming pool known as the Mess Hall, a small club house consisting of a kitchen, a bar room and a dining area. Guests entered through double doors from a gravelled parking area which extended from the roadway beyond the buildings, along the front of the Mess Hall as far as the pool. A walkway of paving stones led around the side of the building, around the pool to the living quarters, which were then only steps away when required.

Towards midnight, Stefan Kristiansson stepped outside the Mess Hall for a breath of air. Inside, the party was in full swing, voices straining to be heard above loud, percussive music, the air thick with marijuana smoke. A strong but thoughtful type, Stefan never felt at home in a scene of wild abandon. He preferred to relax with a drink in a quiet setting, allowing himself to mellow gradually while discussing technical issues with colleagues. Tonight, despite a conscientious effort early on to be sociable, he had gradually faded into the background, and for the last three hours had been slowly and mechanically hoisting one beer after another, uninterrupted at one end of the bar.

He stood entranced by a sense of timelessness, aware only of the whirring of crickets, the pungent aroma of damp, fertile earth, droplets of rain on a leaf caught in a splinter of light from the doorway, and the delicate, leisurely ticking of thorn trees nearby. But as he looked blankly out into the darkness, postponing a decision whether to return to the party or to retire for the night, he suddenly became aware of a figure darting across the road on his left. Shortly afterwards a truck drove out from the compound on the other side.

As a technician, Stefan was not particularly concerned about the movement of company vehicles, but as far as he knew, night shift work was not scheduled to begin until the collar had been completed. He also recognized the truck, from the sound of its engine, as the seven-ton Volvo that Delahaye had driven to Empendwe in the initial convoy. After a moment, without reaching any definite conclusions, he decided on impulse to go back inside.

"Wim!" he called across the room to Van Dyk. "Sweeney's truck has just driven out." As he spoke, he caught sight of Delahaye in the doorway to the kitchen with one of the nurses. The three men looked at one another.

"But I'm right here—how can my truck...?!"

Wim was already at the door, and was just in time to see the vehicle's rear lights disappearing over the hill, a mile to the south. At the same moment, another figure ran across the road, a door slammed, and another truck drove out.

Without waiting for the others, Wim ran to his pickup at the far side of the pool, started the engine and slammed the gearshift into first. As he passed the Mess Hall, Martin sprang out of the doorway and vaulted on to the pickup bed. In his mirror Wim saw Todd and Stefan climbing into another pickup behind him. His wheels spinning on the gravel as he turned on to the road, he floored the accelerator.

Within two minutes they were in sight of the two vehicles and gaining on them. Suddenly, the truck ahead of him swerved to a halt and three men jumped out and ran into the grass. Wim drove off the road in pursuit, and as they drew alongside one of the fugitives, Martin launched himself from the truck, bringing the man down on his face. By the time Wim backed up, Martin had the man in an arm-hold. They trussed him with rope from the back of the cab, heaving him on to the truck bed before backing up on to the roadway.

Todd and Stefan, meanwhile, had followed the first truck down the road, and again the driver had panicked when he realized he could not escape. This time, however, the driver and two others jumped out while the truck was in motion. The vehicle overturned into the ditch, and the men escaped.

They worked into the night, emptying and then righting the overturned truck, bringing back the stolen property and preparing lists for the police. The thieves had emptied most of the storage and office trailers during the party, taking tools, compressors, instruments and the safe, as well as fax, telephone and computer equipment—these last items undoubtedly the most attractive part of the haul since they were new and expensive.

The man they had caught had been taken to a building known as the Fitter's Shop, a long, corrugated iron building which had survived from the original mine, where it had served as a generating station. By this time he had regained his composure, and sat swinging his legs on a bench, grinning at Wim and the others, ignoring their questions.

Unable to make headway, Wim decided to have one of the workers speak to the man. By this time, some of the men had heard the commotion and had come over to see what was going on. At Wim's request, they headed back to their compound and woke up a man sleeping in one of the cabins, a man they called Chaku.

When Chaku reached the Fitter's Shop, he found a number of his co-workers guarding the prisoner. The partygoers, most of whom had not been aware of what was going on, and would not have been vitally interested in any event, had retired for the night, with the exception of the applicants for foreman, who were helping to unload the recovered goods.

Chaku was a wiry man who moved quickly and gracefully, a man who had lived the traditional life of the Lozi people, hunting and fishing along the Kafue River. He was an excellent worker who got on with the job in hand, working productively for hours on end without complaint, although to Wim and others he seemed cold and distant.

Bleary-eyed and partly hung-over, Chaku resented having been routed out of his sleep, and he especially resented the man responsible, this cocksure individual lolling on the bench. This Mavemba.

In his pocket, Chaku had a knife, a wooden affair with a stainless-steel back-loaded spring mechanism. It opened like a standard pocket-knife, but to close the blade it was necessary to slide back a sprung metal strip on the side with the thumb. It was larger than a pocket knife, but served the same purposes.

After staring into the prisoner's eyes for a few frozen seconds, Chaku took out his knife, opened it, stepped forward and in one vicious movement slashed the man's ear off. Before the man had begun to feel the pain, he handed him the ear, then grasped the other one, at the same time saying something to him in a low, husky voice. Suddenly the prisoner began babbling in a high, delirious voice, his face blank with terror. When he stopped, Chaku turned and spoke to two of the men behind him. "Tell the boss we have them," he said.

By seven in the morning, six men, including the original prisoner, were in custody awaiting the police. But the police, Mavembas themselves, were less than enthusiastic about entering Lozi territory, and delayed until the evening. Meanwhile, the workers made the most of their Sunday break, groups of them entering the Fitter's Shop quietly at opportune moments to indulge in an orgy of retribution upon the accused. One man had all his front teeth knocked out of his head with one swipe of an axe, one man had all the fingers of one hand wrenched backwards and broken in a single crunch, most had ribs broken or cracked, and all of them were so severely beaten about the face that by the time the police arrived to take them away, their eyes were tightly-closed slits, their noses so battered that only nostrils were visible, and their features generally reduced to an unrecognizable mass of puffed flesh.

Arriving from Lusaka after dark, the police officers wasted no time. Wim had signed statements ready, together with lists of the items stolen and a provisional estimate of damage to the overturned truck. The six miscreants were escorted into the police wagon, and as they left, one of the officers thanked Wim for calling them.

Later that evening, Wim drove two of the nurses back to Lusaka, while the others drove back with the equipment representative and the other guests. None of the young women had seen the captives, but one, a nurse from Australia, reacted in horror to Wim's description of the punishment they had received. "Are you not responsible," she asked in a voice swelling righteously, "for allowing this to happen while these men were in your custody?"

Wim allowed silence to fall, then laughed quietly. "Welcome to the real world," he said.

5

Selya Paxton came to Lusaka the following Wednesday, aboard the airbus that flew up from Johannesburg twice a week. The flight had taken two hours, arriving at noon. In khaki slacks, a pale blue blouse and a floppy cotton hat, conventional dress calculated to attract as little attention as possible, and carrying a Zambian passport, she passed through Customs without delay.

She had arrived in Johannesburg from London the previous day, and had faxed Wim from her hotel, signing her name "S. Paxton", asking him to meet her at the airport. She knew the mine had been given only the briefest details about her, and was looking forward to seeing his face when it dawned on him that a woman was joining the crew.

She saw him leaning against a telephone cubicle, facing the passengers heading for the exit as he talked, obviously watching for someone. Driven by instinct, she wheeled her suitcase over to the telephones as if to make a call, took an address book out of her purse and leafed through it until she saw him hang up. Then she turned to him and spoke, noticing his eyes relax as he looked at her.

"Excuse me—could you tell me how to get to the Empendwe Mine?"

His expression did not change, but after an interval of perhaps a heartbeat she saw a glint of recognition in his eyes. "You are ...?" he asked, almost as a formality.

"Selya Paxton. And you are Willem Van Dyk."

He laughed, then welcomed her warmly. "Is this all you have?" he asked lightly, reaching for her suitcase and motioning towards the exit doors.

Once they were on the road, he asked her about her experience and how she came to be hired by Anton Turr. Without mentioning her father, and as briefly as possible, she explained that she was a native of Zambia, a geologist by training, and had been looking for an opportunity to return. She had heard of this opening, had applied and had been hired without actually meeting Turr.

In turn, he told her of his upbringing on a farm near Victoria Falls with his father, mother and sister. She listened, and tried to picture him as a boy of five, climbing out of the farmhouse window before dawn to join the little black boys he played with, running with them down to the river, shooting pigeons with a pellet gun, roasting and devouring them on the spot; on Sundays, enduring the fulminations of a Dutch Reform Church minister and the whacks with a sjambok afterwards for forgetting his assigned verses in Sunday School; she pictured him in school, gifted but rebellious, always ready for a fight. Then as a teenager...

He had broken off to point out a line of wattle trees, about two miles ahead, on the crest of a hill. "The mine is just over that rise, to the left of those trees," he told her, glancing at her to be sure she was looking in the right direction, then looking ahead again. She felt his glance linger for an instant, but at that moment she did not feel ready to meet his eyes.

*　　　　　*　　　　　*

Forty miles away, in his office at the Department of National Security, Ben Paxton was scanning the foreign papers, which had just arrived off the morning flight from Johannesburg. As he pored over the previous day's edition of Canada's *National Post*, he reached across the desk and took a stick of biltong from a pewter mug. Holding the shard of spicy cured beef in his left hand, and a knife in his right, he carved towards himself, wrenching a piece off between the blade and his right thumb, then feeding himself from the knife.

Using a marker, he noted news of political or economic developments in countries that provided arms, foreign aid or other assistance either to Zambia or to neighbouring countries. These extracts, together with information retrieved from on-line news services and internal security reports, would be correlated and summarized by his department for his daily briefing of the Prime Minister, the Right-Honourable Virgil Mpetu.

His shaved head gleaming, the veins in his temples pulsating as he chewed, Paxton covered the pages quickly and thoroughly. In the *Financial Post* section, he marked a report of additional incentives for foreign investment in South Africa, which he saw as a sign that economic and political stability was a growing concern in that country, and he noted movements in the price of metals and other commodities. Then he scanned a column of miscellaneous financial news.

The last item in the column read,

> "Cardinal Copper Wire says it has accepted an offer for all of its outstanding common shares at $23.625 a share, from interests represented by the London law firm Bittridge and Druler.
>
> "Toronto-based Cardinal, which makes and distributes copper fittings and extruded tube, said the deal will

provide expansion capital of $70m. for its North American operations."

Paxton stopped chewing and stared at the report. Three thoughts struck him: one, Bittridge and Druler handled the London embassy's legal work; two, the amount of the investment in Canadian dollars was almost exactly fifty billion Zambian kwachas; and three, a shortage of fifty billion kwachas had recently been discovered by the Treasury Department—a shortage the Prime Minister had asked Paxton to investigate personally.

Paxton had suspected immediately that the money was being funnelled into established businesses abroad. Thus legitimized or "laundered", it could be transferred into personal bank accounts or investment portfolios, to be used at will. Laundered money was more difficult to trace than money deposited directly, even into a Swiss bank account.

Money could be laundered in many countries, but because of its stabiltity, its proximity to the United States, and its lenient reporting requirements, Canada ranked among the most preferred destinations. Hence Paxton's attention to the Canadian papers.

The missing funds had been detected during an internal audit which the Prime Minister's Office had abruptly suspended, the team of auditors being disbanded and reassigned to other duties. "I want you to keep this to yourself," Mpetu told Paxton. "Not even your wife must know about it. Our national credibility is at stake. We must get to the bottom of this and deal with it ourselves."

Paxton hesitated. "If I am to investigate something like this," he argued, trying to keep his voice as conversational as possible, "I need at least one man from Treasury and one or two of my own field men." Mpetu had to know, he thought, that one man working alone would never solve the mystery—if there was any mystery to solve.

But Mpetu's expression was becoming homicidal, and Paxton decided to wait. "I'll see what I can do," he said with a shrug, hiding his suspicion.

That night, he had realized that he could either fail to solve the case, or he could find out more than he was meant to find out—more than it was safe to find out. Either way, he would be jeopardizing his position, and his life. In that frame of mind, he had telephoned his daughter and told her to stay away for a while. At least he could try to protect her.

*   *   *

He slowly and carefully folded the newspaper, eased his massive frame from his studded green leather chair, walked briskly across the carpeted office and opened a frosted glass door leading to his secretary's office. Without acknowledging two women working in cubicles along a wall to his right, he crossed to a photocopier, lifted the lid and inserted the newspaper. Having made a copy of the page, he returned to his office and dropped it into his briefcase, then carved himself another piece of biltong and continued scanning the papers.

6

Except for two weeks at Christmas, which was viewed as a break from the heat and humidity and a time to party, work on the collar continued relentlessly until it was finally completed at the beginning of March. Meanwhile, track had been laid from the minehead to the site of the tailings pond, temporary working quarters had been built for the engineers and staff, and a pumping station had been installed. A crew was then able to start cleaning up the old workings—pumping out standing water, hosing down the walls of the vertical shaft and the cross shafts, and shovelling mud and rubble into buckets. This work continued around the clock, and the nocturnal calm was now punctuated every few minutes by the clang of a sledgehammer against a bucket, as its contents were emptied into a trolley.

Half a mile away, Selya listened to this sound as she lay in bed at night, watching the blades of her ceiling fan slowly revolve in the faint light filtering across the pool from the Mess Hall. She loved to listen to the delicate, intimate sounds of nature at night—the sound of raindrops on the windowsill and on the leaves outside, the almost inaudible rustlings of small nocturnal animals, the distant groaning of a puff-adder—but she was comforted as well to be reminded by this mechanical sound that she was not isolated from civilization.

Following Turr's faxed directions, she had spent her first weeks at Empendwe taking ore samples. She had seen at once that she was dealing with someone familiar with her area of expertise. His directions were precise, and he was quick to order a second sample or a re-analysis if there appeared to be any inconsistency within the same area of the site. So far, she was testing only to a depth of thirty feet below the surface, and in effect duplicating the reports Turr had obtained before investing in the mine. Soon, however, she would be able to follow the crews below ground, to test for signs of instability and for underground watercourses.

Earlier that evening, she had joined the men in the Mess Hall, and as they were served by a white-jacketed waiter, she had asked what kind of a yield they expected from this mine.

Wim had speculated that at five thousand feet, the yield might be fifty or sixty per cent copper.

"Fifty per cent more likely than sixty," Stefan replied.

"That's hardly worth it," Selya told him. "We need to be extracting about sixty to break even."

"We could find other minerals when we get down there," Martin suggested. "If we find enough gold…"

Martin had flashed her a smile to let her know he was joking. But Selya was thinking. Why Empendwe? The mine which had been mined out, probably as far as a thousand feet, with only speculative potential below that depth. Why would someone invest a fortune to buy and redevelop this mine?

On the other hand, it was true that smelting technology could now produce a viable yield fom ore which would have been considered useless fifty years ago. Perhaps they would also find that the original workings had not been exhausted. And there was certainly a good chance of finding rich deposits further down.

She eventually dismissed these conflicting thoughts, and fell asleep picturing fossilized trees, exposed by a drilling head, thousands of feet below ground level.

While she was drifting off to sleep, Chaku Melende, who was now in charge of one of the mop-up units, was speaking with Wim Van Dyk in his office. Chaku was reporting that his men had found a rifle two hundred feet down, close to the steps, wedged behind a rail.

Wim looked at the rifle, which was caked with mud, and recognized it as a Martini-action 303, a gun which might have been a relic of the Boer War. His father had kept 303s in the farmhouse, and it was a gun he knew well.

Chaku was asking him for permission to keep the gun. He would leave it with his family in his village, and it would be used only for protection against wild animals.

Wim looked at him closely. He suspected that the gun would be used to shoot game, if anything, but he also knew that it would bring prestige to Chaku's family.

He inspected the gun carefully. Wear and tear had stretched the bolt at the back of the butt, which had become loose, but otherwise there was no obvious sign of damage. He decided to let Chaku have the gun, partly to show appreciation for his hard work, partly in the hope that the gift would make the man less distant.

"I will let you have this gun," he told Chaku, "on condition that you take it to your village as soon as I have cleaned it up for you. It is not to be kept in the compound, or brought to the mine. Do you understand?" His eyes never left Chaku's face.

Chaku nodded quickly, without speaking.

"No guns are allowed at the mine except for the guns I have under lock and key."

Chaku nodded again, his eyes attentive but his expression otherwise inscrutable.

At the end of the shift, Wim took the 303 to the Fitter's Shop and spent two hours making up a new bolt and re-tapping it into the butt. The next day, he thoroughly cleaned and oiled the rifle, then took it out to the slopes to test it; and in the evening, he presented it to Chaku as he came off his shift.

7

They had driven through the long grass down to the Kafue, stopping at the local store in one of the villages. A thatched, mud-walled building like the village huts, the store was equipped with a long counter, behind which canned and packaged foods, flour, sugar, fruit and vegetables were stocked on shelves against whitewashed walls. In addition to staple and sundry items, fish, fowl and game were also generally available at the "location", as Wim called the store.

Half-way back to Empendwe, beside a cluster of rocks jutting from the grass on their right, Wim stopped the pickup. "You can see as far as Kitwe from these rocks," he said, opening the door and getting out.

Selya followed him, and they scanned the horizon beyond the savannah ahead. She drank in the sweet, warm breeze rippling through the grass in front of them, enraptured by the shimmering expanse.

Wim pointed towards a landmark on the horizon, turning towards her as he spoke. As he did so, he caught a flash of her radiant expression and her nubile figure, and a passion overwhelmed him, eclipsing rational thought. He found himself drawn to her, driven by an aching compulsion which could be relieved only by holding her in his arms.

She gasped for breath as he held her, her mind spinning. As she tried to speak, he kissed her, and she felt her heart pounding, her legs weakening. She felt the strength of his arms, his right hand round her waist, his left across her back, holding her head like a baby's, and knew she could not resist.

8

Once the old workings had been cleared, and new lifts and ventilation equipment installed, Selya had holes bored from the lowest level and took samples from depths ranging from ten to one hundred feet. Three weeks later, she received the results by fax from Lusaka. There was copper in every direction—a rich ore body covering about eight thousand square feet, and possibly several hundred feet deep.

"This is incredible," Wim told her. "Why in God's name did they not find this when the mine was worked previously?"

"Their ventilation system may not have worked beyond a thousand feet—I don't know. Or they may have run out of money. Or it may not have been considered safe to go below a thousand feet in this mine for some other reason."

"What though? What could…" He closed his eyes, thinking hard.

She decided not to break his concentration, and let her eyes dwell on his strong, chiselled features. Eventually, he shook his head in frustration and turned to gaze through the windows, across the distant savannah.

Within days, Wim had ordered drilling machines, crushers, additional track and rolling stock, piping of all kinds and dimensions, ladders, wire and hardware, and men were working around the clock, installing equipment as it arrived. Within weeks, the ore body exposed between parallel tunnels running horizontally from the main shaft was being blasted away, carted off, funnelled into buckets and hoisted to the surface to be broken into pieces and pulverized. After being washed through to the leaching plant, where the copper was extracted, the residue, a wet, pasty mud, was piped out to the tailings pond.

About a month after production had begun, the mine recorded its first fatality.

At the eleven-hundred-foot level, holes had been bored and charges set in place, eleven in all, each with fuses hanging down to the floor. The mine had been cleared, except for Martin and Wim, who were at the minehead, Bo Mbolo, the foreman who was checking the charges below, the hoist driver, and a member of the blasting crew, Monde Bilasi.

After a few minutes, the bucket could be heard creaking and whistling its way back up the shaft, and Martin left the office to meet the foreman.

"Boss-boy says we're ready," he called to Wim as he stepped into the bucket. Will nodded and lifted his hand.

Monde was waiting at the crosscut. He and Martin entered the tunnel and found the fuses, set in the wall on their left in a section stretching thirty or forty yards into the tunnel. They agreed that Martin would take the first six, Monde the other five. Each fuse had a time-delay mechanism, and after lighting the ends, they returned to the crosscut and were hoisted back to the surface.

When they arrived, they were met by Mbolo. He had made a mistake: men were still at the bottom of the shaft. "I forget about the sinking crew, sorry, sorry, Bwana," he told Martin, distraught with anguish.

Martin and Monde jumped back into the bucket, which dropped like a stone back to the development section. They raced along the tunnel, ready to slash the fuses with their knives. When he reached his area, Martin found to his relief that none of his fuses had ignited yet. Dancing quickly from one to another, he cut the timers, heaved deeply and called out to Monde, "Okay! You finished?"

"Two more to go," the answer came back from further along the tunnel.

"Okay—see you at the station."

Martin went up to the 1000-foot level to wait.

A few minutes later, he heard a muffled explosion. After calling down the shaft, he climbed back into the bucket and returned to the cross-cut to look for Monde.

Martin smelled smoke in the tunnel, but felt that only one charge could have detonated, otherwise the smoke would have reached the shaft. A single blast would dislodge only a few pounds of rock, so that Monde would have suffered no more than a concussion, if anything.

But the smoke was too thick, and after searching in vain for a few minutes, Martin decided to return to surface and organize a rescue crew. Half an hour later, he had returned to eleven-hundred level with two men, taking a stretcher, lanterns and a first aid kit. They hurried along the tunnel, their footsteps echoing, their shadows leaping up and down against the rock face.

The smoke had cleared when they reached the blasting site, and they hurried on towards Monde's section. Martin passed the first hole, glancing at the fuse and noting the cut end on the ground, then shone his lantern along the wall ahead. "Keep going," he told the other men.

They passed the second, third and fourth holes. In each case, the fuse had been cut. Martin moved on, more slowly now, shining his lantern into the crags and crevices, looking for a human form. His heart was beginning to pound, and he felt a throbbing at the back of his head. But there was still no sign of Monde.

Suddenly, he was stumbling, his lantern flying out of his hand. The two men behind him cried out, and before his hands hit the ground he realized what he had tripped over. Looking back, he saw Monde's body on the ground, about ten feet from the wall. He had taken the full force of the blast, a massive body-blow from the exploding rock, and he had died instantly.

They lifted the limp, shattered body by the coveralls, laid him on a stretcher and brought him back to the surface. After surveying the scene, Wim notified the authorities, telephoning the police in Lusaka, then completing a form to be faxed to the Chief Inspector of Mines. Known as Mines Form 55, the form provided space for a brief account of the accident and a choice of boxes to be ticked, so that the cause of the accident could be indexed by ministry clerks under one of about twenty categories.

The telephone call and the paperwork took Wim less than half an hour. Then he and Martin faced a much harder task: to break the news to Monde's widow.

Taking one of the first-aid clerks with them as an interpreter, they found Monde's village on a plateau overlooking the river, at the end of a footpath which led through the long grass. Leaving their vehicle outside the village, they approached the circle of huts on foot, past a fenced enclosure in which they could see wire-mesh crates of corn, past canoes the villagers would use when the river rose in the rainy season.

A tribesman directed them to one of the huts, and they found Monde's wife in the doorway, braiding the hair of a girl of about five. As they introduced themselves, the woman seemed to retreat into herself, and they could see in her clear brown eyes that she knew instinctively why they had come. They forced themselves to continue, to explain what had happened, telling her of the funeral and death benefits that she would receive, telling her that Monde's body would be brought to her the next day.

They left the village, passing children who had sensed trouble and had stopped playing to watch, passing old men on their three-legged stools, puffing imperviously on pipes of marijuana. They left, trying to shut out the sounds of grief which were beginning to rise behind them, as Monde's family and neighbours began to grasp what had happened.

When Selya went down to eleven-hundred level the next day, Wim was waiting for an investigator from the ministry to arrive, and in the meantime had suspended work in the section. She went alone, knowing that solitude would sharpen her senses, taking with her a lantern, a few of her tools, and some heavy-gauge plastic bags.

At the scene of the explosion, she leant against the opposite wall, then sank down to a sitting position. When her eyes had adjusted to the light, she allowed herself to absorb the evidence—the cavity left in the wall by the explosion, and the debris which fanned out below it. She pictured Monde in his last moments, realizing that he had taken too long to reach his last fuse, hanging back in a sudden panic, then forcing himself to round the curve just as the charge went off. She closed her eyes in a moment of anguish.

Mechanically, she began to scoop up a sample of the debris into one of the plastic bags. As she did so, it struck her that the substance varied in consistency between fragments of rock and a finer, silty material. She stood up, stepped across to the wall cavity, shone her lantern into it, then froze in concentration.

There was a crevice leading upward from the cavity like a chimney. She could see up it about six or seven feet, at which point it seemed to be blocked. At the bottom was a pile of the same silty material she had found on the floor. She scooped some of it into a separate bag, put some rock fragments into another, and returned to surface.

On the way to her office, she saw Stefan and showed him what she had found.

"It looks like pulverized rock—possibly dried tailings," he said. "That's what I was thinking," she replied.

9

Close to the city centre, in a row of buildings that had been residences a hundred years ago, one of Toronto's most exclusive clubs is hidden behind a sombre and anonymous facade. Only on close inspection, as Anton Turr stepped up to the entrance, did he notice the stonemasonry with its interlaced design, the elaborately-carved woodwork and the polished brass initials on the heavy old door, which told him he had found the right address.

"Fraser Chamberlain," he intoned, absorbing at a glance dark wood panelling and a log fire in an iron grate, as an old steward came forward to meet him.

"Mr.Chamberlain will be in the dining lounge, sir, if you would take the elevator to the third floor."

Chamberlain was waiting in a high-backed winged chair near a marble fireplace. As Turr stepped out of the antique elevator, he leaped to his feet, threw his *National Post* on to the chair and came forward eagerly.

"Anton! How are you?" he asked in a tone of earnest sincerity. "How was your flight?"

"I thought this would be quiet, and close to your hotel," he continued quickly, seeing a sour look on Turr's face. "Something to drink?"

"Thank you." Turr said this with a shake of the head.

"You *will* have lunch?"

Turr murmured noncommittally, but allowed Chamberlain to lead the way into the dining room.

"I wanted to explain more fully…"—Chamberlain continued when they were seated, choosing his words carefully, "why we needed you here. There's no problem as far as *we* are concerned, but the reinsurance market is not so easy to handle at the moment."

"I understand." Turr spoke with a hint of impatience. "This is a dangerous investment…"

"Especially when the risk is outside North America."

"…but it is up to us to persuade them otherwise."

"I've explained that this is part of an international account, but they still need some convincing."

Turr inclined his head slightly.

They studied the menu, and Chamberlain wrote their choice on a slip and handed it to a waiter.

"We'll be meeting with reinsurance brokers," he continued.

"They will support this?"

"Well naturally they'd like to place some of the risk, but they have to sell it." He paused while the waiter attended to them. "My hope is that they will find two or three reinsurers willing to take a total of fifty per cent facultatively, in which case our automatic treaty arrangements will bring us up to the ninety-eight per cent we need overall."

"Facultatively?" Turr struggled with the word, giving up after the first three syllables with an expression suggesting he was too bored to continue.

"Arranged specifically for the risk, as opposed to an automatic arrangement."

A streetcar rumbled past below their window. Turr glanced down and across the street at a park awash with flowers.

"You have an assistant with you?" Chamberlain continued.

"I have my engineer, Kristiansson. He is not..." Turr lifted his right hand slightly, his palm facing Chamberlain, in a reassuring gesture.

"Where is he from?"

"He is from Sweden. Mining engineer."

"Got good credentials, has he?"

Turr grunted. "You know Uppsala?" he rumbled. Of course this oaf would know nothing, he was thinking.

"Vaguely..." Chamberlain struggled with his geography. What he really needed to know was that Kristiansson would be a credible witness if it ever became necessary to justify the decision to underwrite the risk.

Over coffee, Chamberlain confirmed with Turr the items of equipment needed for their presentation, and they left to check it out in the boardroom before their visitors arrived.

*   *   *

The reinsurance people had been impressed by Stefan Kristiansson and Anton Turr. After an introduction from Chamberlain, Turr had spoken briefly of his long experience in mining ventures, first as a geologist, then as an investor with an intimate knowledge of world markets. His individuality and striking appearance impressed the brokers as they sipped coffee around the massive mahogany table. A man of Turr's evident international stature *would* be unusual.

Using a desk-top projector, Stefan had addressed the technical details of the survey results at the Empendwe mine, the production targets and projected yields. Clearly an expert in his field, his enthusiasm had inspired confidence.

After the presentation, both men had answered questions clearly and succinctly. Turr, in particular, with a masterful combination of patience and disdain, had handled a question about profitability from an executive of the brokerage who had failed to grasp what had been said earlier, leaving his audience impressed and slightly humbled. Finally, everyone had been provided with a copy of the technical reports, and a report from a firm of accountants in London that addressed projected values of production at the mine over the coming three years. Turr and Kristiansson had then returned to their hotel, leaving Chamberlain to close the meeting with a short statement to the effect that it seemed clear to everyone that the Empendwe mine was a viable enterprise with a very promising future, and that reinsurers were looking at a very desirable risk in the circumstances. The values provided supported coverage for property and profits of one hundred million at current exchange rates, to be part of the existing schedule of Anton Turr's international holdings, and the brokerage was invited to place fifty percent facultatively. There had been no dissent.

*   *   *

Flying Business Class to Grand Cayman, the two men savoured their drinks and gazed out on to the clouds below. Both were satisfied with their performance in Toronto. Stefan felt that the experience had broadened his horizons, while Turr saw his plans advancing on schedule. Both were ready to celebrate and relax, and as Turr threw back one vodka after another, Stefan followed suit.

While giving no indication that the vodka was affecting him, Turr gradually became more communicative than usual, his voice dropping into a confidential tone. "I see many mines, many years," he rumbled. "Russia, Canada, Africa, South America, I know all these mines." He waved his hand in a sweeping gesture, then continued, "You people at Empendwe mine—you are my best team. Any time in future you need help, you need reference, you need work in my organization, you come to me. I will take care of it."

Stefan thanked him warmly, and then, feeling somehow that he should balance the euphoria, raised the subject of Monde Bilasi's recent death.

"I received report," Turr said.

Stefan mentioned Martin's quick action, which he considered heroic, in going down and cutting the fuses to save the sinking crew from suffocating. "But we can't understand how Monde took so long to cut his ends," he said.

Turr grunted thoughtfully. "This, I have seen before, many years," he said. "When I was working in Kazakh. Now, this is electric…electronic…"

"Some mines still use the old fuses," Stefan told him. "Some of the men think they are more reliable."

"They are receiving bonus?"

"Yes."

"So, they like to start the fuses themselves. Is more reliable to them. I understand." He lifted his glass to signal for a refill.

"In Kazakhstan, were you mining copper?" Stefan asked.

"Copper, iron ore. Zinc, one mine."

Stefan tried to imagine life under the old Soviet regime. "Were you posted to Kazakhstan after university?"

"No. I was five years in northern Urals. Copper, nickel, iron."

"Kazakhstan would have better yields of copper, I think."

Turr nodded. He began to recite the types of minerals found in the Urals. Kazakhstan had less variety, but greater productivity.

Stefan was curious how Turr had begun to build his empire of mines and properties. But Turr seemed unwilling to be drawn out. "After communism, everything was possible," was all he would say.

Stefan then remembered the debris Selya had showed him. "Something else we found," he said, leaning forward slightly, "—there was some old, dried silt in a cavity in the foot wall. Selya showed it to me. I thought it looked like tailings."

He did not see Turr's eyes narrow. After a moment, Turr asked, "You have samples?"

"Yes—Selya took samples. Maybe she will have some results by now."

After a silence, Turr said, "I will look into it." He closed his eyes and tilted his seat back, seeming to retreat into himself. But ten minutes later, when Stefan thought he had fallen asleep, Turr was suddenly thrusting his glass towards the stewardess, using his elbow as he did so to urge Stefan to join him in another round.

When they had been served, Turr lifted his glass in salutation, then drank. "I have been thinking," he said. "There is some work you can do for me, on Cayman Islands."

Stefan was pleasantly surprised. Turr had invited him to his island for a few days' vacation as a reward for his performance in Toronto, and as a break from his work at Empendwe. A special assignment would be an additional privilege. "I am happy to help," he replied.

"I will give you details tomorrow," Turr continued. "You can stay a few weeks, if necessary." He looked at Stefan as if expecting a reply, but before Stefan could speak, he added, "I will make arrangements with Van Dyk."

10

Paxton pushed through a scrum of reporters at the entrance to the Ministry of Mines and Natural Resources, crossed the marble foyer and ran up the carpeted steps, past police and security officers who stood aside to let him pass. On the next level, at the end of a corridor to his right, he was saluted by an officer. Paxton identified him by his gold cap crest as a member of the presidential guard. The officer opened a door, waited for Paxton to enter, then closed it behind him.

The door led to a reception room, beyond which Paxton heard the sound of voices. Moving quickly, he crossed the empty room and opened a door on the other side.

Paxton recognized the three men in the room: Clarence Tibuluma, Chief of the National Police Force, Deputy Chief David Forster, and Deputy Minister Francis Mangola. All three glanced at him as he entered, but no greetings were exchanged.

"Where is he?" Paxton asked, speaking to the three men as a group.

"The Minister is at the Lusaka General Hospital," Mangola said in a sibilant whisper. "Not expected to live."

Paxton took a Queen Anne chair from a corner of the room near the door, and brought it over to the desk behind which Mangola was seated. "Do you have a suspect?" he asked Tibuluma.

"Not at the present moment," the Chief answered ponderously. "We are hoping the Minister will regain consciousness."

"Were there no other witnesses?"

The Chief shifted his enormous rump and shot a glance in Paxton's direction. "We are questioning everybody," he said.

"I'd like to see the crime scene," Paxton said brusquely, getting to his feet. "David?"

Forster glanced at Tibuluma, and seeing no reaction stood up and moved towards the door to join Paxton.

Paxton led the way back across the reception area and into the corridor. Near the centre of the building, he turned right, up a stairway to the next floor, too impatient to wait for the elevator alongside. Forster, a tall, lean man with hard-bitten features, strode briskly behind him. At the top of the stairs, the corridor was cordoned off and manned by officers, who made way, saluting both men as they passed. At the end of the corridor they entered a long, deeply-carpeted room, at the end of which, above a grand piano, hung a portrait of Virgil Mpetu. On their left, leading from a doorway near the piano and ending abruptly in the middle of the carpet, was a trail of blood.

"There were no witnesses?" Paxton asked again.

"None that we know of."

"Who is being questioned?"

"Everybody who was in the building at the time. Amanda was at lunch. Lilya had the day off. They are both at home."

Paxton made a mental note to speak to the secretaries himself. "How many people heard shots?"

"Only one shot was heard. The Minister was only hit once, in the chest."

"Who found him?"

"Grace Ngela, when she brought his lunch at one o'clock. Apparently he'd been shot a few minutes before that, but the people who heard it were all on the far side of the building. They weren't sure what they'd heard at that point."

"Was the Minister conscious when he was found?"

"No."

"Has the bullet been extracted—can we establish the calibre?"

"Not calibre—gauge. It was a shotgun wound."

"A shotgun!" Paxton stared incredulously at the deputy chief. "And the assassin got out of the building without being seen?"

"He would have had time to pack it into a case. We have no idea at this point what he did with it."

Paxton thought for a minute. He was standing at the doorway to the minister's office, noting that the trail of blood led to the desk opposite. "Let's go back," he said eventually.

Tibuluma and the Deputy Minister were still in the office downstairs. "I'm going to see the Prime Minister," he told Tibuluma. "Please let me know as soon as you get any leads."

There was no response. Both men were inscrutable.

II

Surrounded by blue, rippling water, the Cayman Islands sparkled with colour, the bright green foliage dotted with pink, orange and white roofs. As the plane made its descent, Stefan could see the white sails of yachts near the beach, and as they approached the runway, he saw men stacking cardboard boxes on a barge, throwing them from one man to the next in a relay.

They left the terminal after clearing customs, and headed back across the tarmac towards a hangar in which Turr's helicopter was waiting. Within ten minutes they were airborne over dense bush punctuated by shacks and smallholdings. Soon they were over water again.

"There is my island," said Turr, pointing ahead into the setting sun. Stefan saw the outline of hills rising from the sea, clothed in soft folds of foliage, now in shade, an orange-yellow gleam of sunlight beginning to dip behind them. As they came closer, he could make out the shapes of the hollows and ravines that etched the hills, and he saw the outline of a stream falling in a broken line to the white foam edging the shore.

When they were within half a mile of the island, a white speck deep in the hills began to take shape as a chateau, and when Turr turned and banked the helicopter to clear the trees, Stefan saw a cluster of buildings surrounding a courtyard, in the centre of which was a landing pad.

As they climbed out, they were met by a steward in a white jacket who collected their luggage. A man in coveralls got into the cockpit and began to taxi the helicopter towards a hangar at the back of the courtyard.

Followed by Stefan and the steward, Turr led the way through an archway to a gravelled path skirting the front of the property, overlooking the sea. The tropical warmth relaxed Stefan, and he felt exhilarated by the beauty of the island and its isolation from the rest of the world.

The path led to a white cottage nestling among palm and hibiscus trees. As the steward opened the door and carried Stefan's suitcase inside, Turr stopped and said, "Anything you need, you can call Aaron. He will give you the number. Please come to the house in the morning at six o'clock. I will explain the work I want you to do here."

Stefan thanked him and followed Aaron inside. The cottage was nicely furnished, with a living room, a kitchen and two bedrooms. The doors to the bedrooms were open, and he could see a bed with crisp white sheets turned down in one of the rooms.

Aaron gave him a slip of paper. "Here is the extension to call, sir, if you need anything."

Stefan thanked him, warming to the man's lilting accent. The soft, musical tone added to his euphoria, and he regressed subconsciously to his boyhood in Sweden, when the sound of his grandparents' voices, also soft and lilting, had given him a similar sense of calm and belonging.

After unpacking and showering, he took a beer outside and leant over the stone wall fronting the pathway. The ground below fell away steeply, and he looked down in the moonlight over the treetops and out to sea. A slight breeze stirred scents of wild roses and nutmeg, while the soft lapping of the surf below was the only sound to caress the night air. When he eventually returned to the guesthouse and retired for the night, the primordial rhythm of the surf drew him instantly under its spell, into a deep, contented sleep.

He awoke once during the night, aware of moonlight so bright it was surreal. Almost immediately he drifted back to sleep, but in that instant he felt he had seen a face at the window: the face of a woman.

As always, he awoke before dawn, and shortly after half past five left the guesthouse to look around before his appointment with Turr. Outside, the air was cool, and he could almost taste the fresh dew on the leaves. Birds were beginning to stir, and the first rays of the rising sun lit up the water directly ahead. He followed the path towards the courtyard, then continued towards the other side of the property, eventually reaching the stream which he had seen from the helicopter. As he approached it he could hear the rush of water, and in a building nearby, the sound of generating equipment.

The path and the wall ended at this point, the wall curving to join the end of the building. Stefan looked over the wall, and saw that the stream below zig-zagged away for about a hundred yards before falling to the sea.

It was now five minutes to six, and he retraced his steps quickly, back to the archway that led into the courtyard, then across to the mansion on the other side.

It was a two-storied building, white, with a wide entrance framed by columns rising from a terrace of terra-cotta tiles up to a classic apex. On either side of the central structure, and recessed slightly from it, were symmetrical wings, each with three tall leaded windows on both levels. A gravelled pathway bordered by palm trees, with a fountain at its mid-point, led to the entrance.

Stefan walked up the tiled steps to the front door, a double door flanked by panes embedded with brass and wrought-iron leaves.

Almost as soon as he rang the bell, the door opened and he was welcomed by Aaron, who led him across a large, square entrance hall into a study in the East wing. "I shall be serving breakfast later, sir," Aaron said, "but would you care for coffee now?" He inclined his head towards a tray set on a desk covered in dark green leather.

Stefan accepted with thanks, and was savouring the most exquisite coffee he had ever tasted when he became aware that Turr was standing behind him, watching silently. Before he could move, he felt an enormous hand on his shoulder, which he took as an indication that he was to remain at ease. Nothing was said, and Turr moved behind the desk as Aaron poured him a cup of black coffee.

Turr drank his coffee, his face in shadow. Eventually, he said, "Yesterday, I told you, I have work for you here. My computer…I have expert operator, but she knows nothing about mines." Aaron refilled his cup.

"Is necessary to provide complete report to the government of Zambia. Now, we operate the old mine, but the old mine is nothing. In two years, we mine ten thousand feet. We have new mine." He swallowed his coffee in a single gulp.

"Government Chief Inspector…is necessary to approve plans. Old workings, new workings. Also, complete report of equipment, production procedure, facilities. I will show you reports for other mines I have—Canada, South America, Russia—you will see them."

"You will do this here. Any information you need, the mine will fax here. When complete, I will approve and take to the government. While you are here, the assistant you train…"

"Ulame."

"…he will take over your work at the mine."

Stefan was overcome by gratitude. He was flattered to be trusted with such an important assignment. He was also intoxicated by the beauty and isolation of the island, and by the luxury of the surroundings.

Turr stood up. "Now I will show you your office, and some reports which will be a guide for you," he said. "Also the girl, Anita. She will come down later."

12

On the third day after the shooting, the Minister died without regaining consciousness, and the next day, a shotgun was found amongst painters' supplies near a loading dock at the rear of the building. Earlier in the day, maintenance staff had seen a man loitering near the wooden steps at the side of the dock, as if looking for an opportunity to find his way inside.

"I could see that the gun had to have been brought in the back way," Paxton told Mpetu, explaining how he had narrowed the focus of the search. "Either by a workman, or somebody masquerading as one. So he could move around without attracting attention."

Mpetu's dark face was set hard in concentration, and he seemed poised to spring out from behind his desk. "Evidently it was someone masquerading," he said. "No doubt the same man who was seen this morning. It was not very clever of him to come back to try to get it."

"Very stupid. But it was obviously something he wanted to keep."

"What was he?"

"The people who saw him recognized him as a Lozi. So far, that's all…"

A glint of understanding flashed across Mpetu's face. "I want him found," he said with controlled ferocity. "And when he is found, I wish full particulars, why he did it, who was behind it. You will *make* him speak."

<h1 style="text-align:center">13</h1>

They lay together, oblivious of time, aware only of the constant whirring of crickets in the darkness outside. The sound seemed to pulsate to a regular rhythm, as if a myriad of insects were performing in concert.

Casually, he slid his arm under her and pulled her to him, feeling the padded softness of her back and the doll-like contours of her shoulders. His passion returned, driving him with an irresistible force, and as he took her she felt herself locked in an iron grip, launched on a journey in which she participated with only a token struggle for physical and emotional control.

Half an hour later, the telephone rang. A man had arrived at the mine on foot from his village on the Kafue River, with an axe embedded in his skull. Morag Cuthbert, the resident nurse, was calling Wim to the First Aid centre.

The axe was a villager's standard equipment, as ubiquitous as a pocket-knife. Of great antiquity, it consisted of a thin wedge of pig iron fitted into a slot in a handle usually carved from a root or branch of the mapani tree. The slot would be burned into the bulbous end of the handle by the back of the axe head itself, a laborious process in which the iron was repeatedly heated and ground into the wood, ensuring a perfect fit. Using the axe rammed the head even more tightly into the slot, but the head could be knocked out by striking the back of the axe against a rock or tree, and it then became a versatile hand tool, useful for filletting and flaying, or for paring bark. The handle tended to be shaped into a curve at the top, setting the axe head in a slight crook which fit nicely over a man's shoulder, the handle against his chest.

The man came to Empendwe knowing that there were people there who could tend to his injuries. After his wife had unexpectedly brought the axe down on his head, he had staggered through the village and out on to the Flats. Bleeding freely down his face and neck, pain shooting through his head in violent spasms, he had kept moving mechanically until he reached the mine.

Walking into the general office, he had stood there in complete silence. The first-aid clerk on duty had summoned Morag, and in the meantime had led the victim into the clinic. When Wim arrived, the man was still standing, slightly stooped, as if balancing the axe on his head.

Wim approached to take a closer look, placing one hand on the man's shoulder. Morag and the clerk threw up their hands convulsively, afraid that he might touch the axe. He reassured them with a gesture, and turned to Morag.

"There is nothing you can do here?"

"No. Apart from morphine, nothing. And that might be the wrong thing to do in this case." She spoke with a clipped Scottish accent.

"Then please take him to hospital in the ambulance," he told her, asking Sam, the clerk, to drive. He felt the three other first-aiders could handle routine injuries for a few hours. The managers and foremen also had first-aid certificates, as required by the mining regulations.

Sam drove the first twenty-five miles slowly over the dirt road, knowing that every rut, every stone, could jar the axe free and cause fatal hemorrhaging. The final eighteen miles, on a tarred surface, were easier, but by then the patient, seated on a padded bench, was being held upright by Morag. On arrival at the hospital, he was already dead.

The hospital administrator reported the apparent manslaughter to the police as routine procedure. Since the dead man, a tribesman from the Kafue, carried no identification, the administrator expected simply to be told to cremate the body and file a death certificate. When he mentioned that the man had been brought from Empendwe, however, a long silence at the other end was followed by a peremptory "Stay on the line, please" barked into the receiver. Eventually, he was told that officers would be at the hospital shortly, and that the driver and the nurse should wait for them.

An hour later, two plain-clothes officers entered the main lobby, flashed their identification and asked for the administrator. An urgent telephone call brought him hurrying down from his third-floor office, together with the two mine employees. After a short exchange, the administrator led the way to a private room close by. He was then waved away by one of the officers, who used the back of his hand for this purpose while ushering the pair from Empendwe into the room with the palm of the same hand.

"Do you know who we are?" one of the officers asked as soon as they were seated. He himself, apparently the more senior of the two, had taken his position behind a desk. He was heavily built, overweight, wearing a multi-coloured, loose-fitting shirt. The question was asked with an exaggerated smile which stretched the man's closely-cropped moustache until sweat glistened between the stubble.

There was no answer, and he continued, "I am Detective-Sergeant Ola. This is Detective Simbra. We are from the Department of National Security."

The employees stiffened. Morag clasped her hands together in her lap, and Sam gripped the sides of his chair.

"We only have a few questions," Ola continued. "About the man you brought here tonight." He smiled again, radiantly, apparently for his own pleasure.

"Tell me about this man. How long had he been working at the mine." The last sentence was spoken flatly and without inflection, although grammatically it was a question .

Morag spoke first. "We had never seen him before. He apparently walked from the Kafue, from his village."

Ola looked at her for a long time. Then he turned to Sam. "Your name is?" he asked.

"Samuel Lemenga, sir."

"How long have you been working at the Empendwe mine?"

"Two years, sir."

"The dead man, what was his name?"

"He never spoke his name. He never spoke at all."

Ola turned and spoke quietly in his dialect to his colleague. Then he turned back to the mine employees and said abruptly, "We are charging you with obstruction of an official investigation. We will continue this conversation at D.N.S. headquarters." He stood up, motioning to Simbra, who drew a gun from a holster on his belt and moved quickly behind Morag and Sam. Despite Morag's protests, both were handcuffed and taken out through the lobby to a chauffeur-driven Mercedes, with DNS plates, waiting at the entrance.

14

Wim put down the telephone, left his office and strode towards his pickup. He was holding the top of the driver's door, shouting an explanation to Martin, when Selya ran towards him.

"I'm going with you." She opened the passenger door.

"I can handle it."

"No! Please. I'll explain."

He looked at her searchingly, then got in and started the engine. As he spun the pickup around, he looked at her again but said nothing.

"Wim, I heard what you were telling Martin. I can help."

"I've bailed out employees before."

"You know this isn't a routine matter. I heard you mention the DNS."

"I can handle them."

"Wim, no! You know that isn't realistic. If the DNS are involved, it's madness to interfere."

"I'm responsible for sending Morag and Sam to Lusaka, and I have to get them back."

"Wim, my father is chief of the DNS. Let me see him. It's the only…"

He stopped the pickup and turned to look at her. "Why didn't you...?"

"It didn't matter until now. There was no need to mention it."

He rested his forehead on the steering wheel. After a minute, he put the pickup in gear and drove forward again.

They drove another mile before Selya spoke again. "Wim?" she said quietly.

"Later."

They reached the city by 9.30, passing local vendors on the highway, their brightly-coloured cloth, carvings, hand-made jewellery, fruit and vegetables displayed on stands along the wide grassy median. They took Livingstone Road to Leopard's Hill Road, passing the police headquarters and the Lusaka Hotel and continuing up the hill to the State House.

At the entrance to the grounds, Wim asked for the Government Mining Engineer's office, and was waved through into the parking lot. "They've seen me before," he told Selya. "They expect me to be here on mining business, and it saves time to let them think that."

They walked up the steps, through the ornate entrance doors into a spacious marble foyer. Directly ahead, a broad stairway swept upwards, bronze railings fanning out at the top in each direction. A security officer sat behind a desk in an alcove at the foot of the stairs.

"Wait here," she told Wim, firmly rejecting his attempts to argue. She went to the security desk, spoke to the officer and waited as he made a telephone call.

"Colonel Paxton is in a meeting, ma'am," he said after hanging up. "But his secretary will tell him you're here." He motioned to her to take a seat, and she sat near Wim on an adjacent bench.

Ten minutes later, the burly figure of the Chief of National Security came bounding down the stairs, a wary expression on his face. Selya came forward to meet him, as if to embrace. "Not here," he told her quickly, keeping his voice down.

Wim got to his feet, but Selya held up her hand. Paxton glanced at Wim, then told Selya to follow him.

"What in God's name are you doing here?" he asked her after closing his office door. "I told you it isn't safe here."

"Daddy—this is still my country. And if you are in trouble, I want to be here."

"How long have you been here?"

"A year…a year and a half."

"So you were deceiving me."

"I did arrange to have cards and things sent from London. I'm sorry. But I didn't want you to know where I was. I was offered a very good position here."

"At an old mine on the Kafue Flats."

"You knew."

"Of course I knew. I knew the day you arrived. I get a list of everyone who comes into the country. Naturally your name stood out a mile. But I decided not to risk making contact. I knew where you were. I could get you out if I had to."

"I don't want to cause any problems. I thought if you were in trouble, I could ask Professor Arnald…"

"Arnald has already got a message to me about undercover operatives ready to help. I appreciate the thought. But the chance that these messages and contacts may be intercepted only makes life more dangerous."

"I'm so sorry." Tears in her eyes, she put her arms around him.

Paxton did not move. "We can't afford to be sentimental. Obviously you need my help now. What do you want me to do?"

"The mine has a nurse and a first-aid clerk who brought an injured man to the General Hospital yesterday night. They haven't returned, and the hospital told us this morning that they were taken away by D.N.S. men."

Paxton moved behind his desk. His expression had become severe.

"Your people are all right," he said. "They have told us what we needed to know."

"Can we take them back?"

"It isn't as simple as that. First of all, they have been charged with withholding evidence in a murder investigation."

"But the man already had the axe in his head when he arrived at the mine."

"We don't know that. It's unlikely that he walked seven miles in that condition. But we're not talking about him—we're talking about the murder of Mr. Latonga." He watched his daughter's reaction.

"How could they possibly have had anything to do with that?"

"Somebody at Empendwe did. We have the weapon, and we think a Lozi was involved, which gives us the geographical area. The weapon was an antique shotgun, which probably came from an old mine. The motive may have been partly tribal, but the choice of the Minister of Mines and Natural Resources is another factor."

"There are dozens of mines in the Copper Belt."

"Antique 303s are unlikely to turn up in a modern mine."

"It's still only speculation."

"That's how we make progress. We piece together information, we look for coincidences and clues, we follow a line of thought. Call it speculation, but that's why we are successful. That's why the case was transferred to my department. Tibuluma was getting nowhere—as usual."

"But how could our first-aid people have known anything about it?"

"It turned out that the clerk knew about the gun. We got that out of him…"

"Did you hurt him?" Her voice was low, but with a hint of the dread she was feeling.

Paxton looked at her with a mixture of curiosity and impatience. "We rely on our reputation," he told her. "There's a lot of folklore about the D.N.S., which helps to loosen tongues. It helped in this case."

"But can't you release the employees? Surely the nurse knew nothing."

"You'll have to be patient while we sort everything out." There was no point in explaining that the accomplices, or the mastermind, if any, might now be in a state of panic at the thought that witnesses were undergoing prolonged interrogation, and would reveal anything to end the ordeal. It was psychological gamesmanship. The culprits might now draw attention to themselves by trying to run, or they would be ready to crack by the time they were brought in for questioning. Either way, his job would be easier.

"I can give you this much," he said after a pause, seeing the pain on his daughter's face. "The clerk told us that the shotgun had been found down the mine. He saw a man firing it on the Flats, spoke to this man, and this was what he was told. We showed him the gun, and he identified it by a new butt bolt.

"He thought the man who had the gun had also found it. He had no idea how it came to have a new butt bolt. These points need to be investigated. If somebody else fixed up this gun for the assassin, he is in very serious trouble." He watched her reaction.

Selya said nothing. She felt disturbed. Her father had been open with her, but despite this, everything had become unclear and uncertain. Intuitively, she felt he knew more than he was saying.

After a while, Paxton spoke again. "I can only help so far. Our investigation of accomplices or accessories can be delayed while we concentrate on finding the assassin. In the meantime, we keep this meeting to ourselves. Any of my staff who see you leaving can think you were here to talk about job opportunities. When you leave, walk straight out without speaking to anybody. And by the way, your people are not behind bars—they are in protective custody down the road, at the Lusaka Hotel."

15

Stefan had been reading technical reports for about two hours when he heard a voice behind him, looked round quickly and caught sight of a young woman in white shorts and a pale yellow halter top. To give himself time to collect his thoughts, he threw down the papers he had been studying, clapped his right hand on the desk in front of him and heaved himself energetically to his feet.

She was smiling at him, a hint of worldliness in her eyes tempering the shock of her beauty. "You must be Anita," he said stiffly. "I look forward to working with you here."

Smiling more radiantly, she said, "I will explain the computer to you."

She moved towards a panelled alcove, tapped in a code and pressed a button. A lock clicked, and a section of the panelled wall slid open to reveal a computer room, about eight feet square and windowless, in which Stefan could make out a bank of computer terminals. He followed her into the room, becoming aware of the low hum of ventilation equipment.

"This is the mainframe. It is hooked up to Mr. Turr's financial enterprises all over the world," she told him.

He nodded, noticing her dark, luxuriant hair, which fell almost to her waist, and marvelling at the clarity of her light brown eyes.

He swallowed and said, "I need only to access production and yield reports from the Empendwe mine, and interface with the management and engineers there."

"I will give you a password and the code to this room. I will also set you up on E-mail. You will have everything you need. Sit here, please."

He caught a fresh scent on her hair as she leant over his shoulder to enter the access codes, displaying her slender arms and manicured nails. She was wearing a slim gold wrist watch, but no rings.

"You are in," she said brightly, giving him a note of his password and the procedures he would need to follow.

"I may need some help in layout and editing," he told her, turning to face her.

"Don't worry—I am here. If I am not in here, I am in Mr. Turr's office."

He listened to her speech, and thought it sounded different from Aaron's. "Do you live here?" he asked her.

She laughed. "My home is in Ecuador," she said. "But I am here now, since two years." She started to leave the computer room.

"Where is Mr. Turr's office?" he called out.

"On the second floor." She gestured elegantly towards the west wing.

He returned to the office and continued reading the sample reports, making notes as he progressed. After a while, he opened a casement window and caught the scent of bougainvillea and magnolia blossoms. Two young men whom he had seen climbing out of the helicopter earlier were tending to the landscaping around the courtyard.

At noon, Aaron brought him sandwiches and coffee, and half an hour later, Turr came into the room. "I have understanding with government inspector in Zambia," he said. "You are working on report, will finish in three months."

Stefan thanked him, and briefly considered offering to do better. After a moment's hesitation, he said, "I think that is possible."

Turr looked at him with a hint of curiosity, then said, "Anita— she needs friend, I think. I am older. You work together with her, get to know better."

When Aaron came for the tray an hour later, he said, "I shall bring your evening meal to your guest house at seven, sir. And I understand from Mr. Turr that you will have a guest this evening, sir."

16

They left the State House quickly, drove back to the Kafue-Lusaka Road and stopped beside a stonemason's yard. Wim crossed his hands on the top of the steering wheel and rested his head on them.

"Do you think you should see a lawyer?" she asked him.

He said nothing for a while. "I only know corporate lawyers," he said eventually, his voice low and emotionless.

"We need advice." She spoke softly but insistently.

After a minute, he looked up. "I had a lawyer who took care of a hunting charge for me," he said. "The time I shot a warthog."

"Why not at least speak to him?"

"I'm trying to remember his name. Roger..." He pressed his wrist to his forehead.

"Try..."

"Roger Chilonga. He should be in the telephone directory." He started the engine and drove back into Lusaka.

They found the offices of Kemp and Chilonga in a building called Samefa House, just off Livingstone Road. A receptionist told them that Mr. Chilonga was in court, but might return during an adjournment. They sat down to wait.

An hour later, a man in barrister's robes and white tie opened the door. His expression was still alert and watchful, as if ready for the unexpected counter-attack or rebuttal, and his eyes covered the waiting room without blinking.

Wim stood up and reached for Chilonga's hand. "Roger, I'm Wim Van Dyk. You acted for me a while ago," he said, as Chilonga shook his hand cordially.

"Yes, yes! And what can I do for you now—please come in," he said loudly, leading the way into his office and dropping his tall frame into the chair behind his desk.

"This is my colleague, Selya Paxton." There was a flicker of recognition.

"By the way," Chilonga said, still in an orator's voice, "I do not take clients direct…"

"Roger, this is an emergency." Wim's voice was quiet but urgent. "I have no-one else to turn to."

Chilonga's expression became serious.

"All I need is a yes or no," Wim continued.

Chilonga looked at him closely. "Tell me," he said.

Wim explained how he had been implicated in the assassination. When he had finished, the barrister swivelled round in his chair and stared out of the window. After a few moments, he folded his arms and turned to face Wim.

"This is a very high-profile case." He paused to make sure his point was taken. "The Government regards the assassination as a direct attack on their authority. They will make an example of anyone implicated in it."

"If the victim had been less prominent, you would have nothing to fear. There is no evidence that you had any motive, any previous problems with the ministry, any connection with elements who might have plotted the assassination. You would testify that you simply gave this man the gun as a gift to be used for hunting only, and you would be believed."

"Even then, you would be guilty of failing to register the gun. But that is a minor misdemeanor." He waved his hand in a dismissive motion. "I would have no difficulty in getting a suspended sentence on that count."

"However, the situation we are facing now is that an assassin took the gun and shot the minister. Had you not given him the gun, if you had not given it to him in working order, or if you had made sure that the gun was registered, the assassination might not have taken place. You made it easy for him to carry out his plan, because he was presented with a gun in working order, and one which he might think would never be traced."

"A court would probably find that by doing this, you aided and abetted the assassin. You would probably be found to have been an accessory to murder." He stopped to allow his words to take effect.

Wim spoke slowly, his voice flat. "What sentence could I expect to receive?" he asked.

"I would expect twenty-five years". He sounded detached, as if speculating on a technical matter. "However," he added, "you might get the death penalty."

Selya had been listening to Chilonga's voice, following the drift of his argument and sensing that he was leading to an unwelcome conclusion. Through the window behind him, she could see a blue-headed lizard moving along a branch of a jacaranda tree. As Chilonga concluded his monologue, his words reached her through a haze of denial.

In a moment, her strength of mind had returned, and she noticed Wim, tense and silent beside her. "We have to leave the country," she said quietly.

Wim looked at her, but said nothing.

Chilonga looked at them thoughtfully. "Let me give you some advice," he said. "But first, you understand that this meeting has not taken place." He waited for them to murmur their assent. "If you leave Zambia, my advice is not to take the road. They may be watching the borders. Your picture may also be on the wanted lists in the police stations, and they may already be at the mine. You will do better to take a plane. A commercial flight. But do not wait long."

He stood up and held out his hand. "Good luck."

17

Stefan listened to the muffled sounds of wildlife echoing through the trees, and to the surf caressing the shore below in the stillness before dawn. The pure air on his body heightened his sense of ecstasy. He felt he was eavesdropping on the intimate sounds and rhythms of nature, an eternal melody almost beyond human comprehension.

After a while, he drew himself out of his reverie, and returned to his cottage, to the nubile young woman who now shared his bed.

In the morning, he worked on his report, entering and printing pages as he progressed. Anita came to the computer room twice during the morning, leaning seductively over to collect the sheets, and it took all his will-power to resist her temptation.

Shortly before noon, the computer flashed an E-mail notice. Stefan called up the message and read, "Have to be away for a while. Will try to keep in touch. Van Dyk."

He began to reply, asking for more details. But before he could finish, Anita rushed breathlessly into the room, sat down at the centre console and tapped rapidly at the keyboard. Then she hurried out without a word.

Stefan completed and dispatched his message to Van Dyk, but was confronted with the phrase, "Receiver ID suspended". He tried to reach Martin, Todd, Selya and his assistant Ulame, but with the same result.

He sensed that Turr had made some changes at the mine, but hesitated to interrupt him by calling or going up to his office. He thought he might wait until they met casually before raising the subject. He could then avoid appearing too curious or demanding, and in the meantime might receive an explanation without having had to ask.

But there was no word from Turr. After lunch, he walked around the courtyard, then up and down the gravel path beside the wall outside. When he came back half an hour later, he decided on impulse to go up to Turr's office, as if casually looking round during his lunch break.

A white staircase, carpeted with a wine-coloured runner, curved upwards from the left side of the entrance hall. Climbing the stairs, Stefan had almost reached the top when he heard Turr's voice. He hesitated for a moment, then thought he heard Turr mention his name. Turning his head towards the voice, he saw a door ajar about six feet to his left. He moved closer, and caught some disjointed words and phrases between long silences.

"He can not get…"

"We are already…"

"…will be filed before three months…"

"…a few months…a year…"

Turr's voice kept fading, then recovering, and Stefan decided that he must be walking around with the telephone. He could make no sense of what he heard, but suddenly felt that being there was a mistake. He turned to go back down the stairs, but as he did so he saw Aaron standing in the hallway, looking up at him.

He had no idea how long Aaron had been watching him, and began to feel furtive. Annoyed with himself, he ignored Aaron, continued up to the landing, and knocked on the door to Turr's office.

He heard a grunt, then felt a muffled tread approaching. The door opened quickly, and he saw Turr looking down at him with an ugly expression.

18

Wim carefully removed some of the debris at the entrance to the adit. Working his head and shoulders inside, he shone a flashlight into the tunnel. He saw that the roof had collapsed about ten yards from the entrance, but the timbers up to that point looked sound. He eased himself through the gap and checked the time: 2 a.m.

Inside, he reached back for a sports bag he had brought with him, containing tools, a jug of water, a hard hat, overalls, work gloves, a breathing mask and food. He set the bag down behind the debris at the entrance.

The tunnel was small, not much more than seven feet wide and about the same height. There were no tracks, and no electrical conduit on the walls or ceiling. He decided that the tunnel had once been an auxiliary route out of the mine, provided to comply with regulations, but never used for regular traffic.

Wim moved forward carefully, testing the supports, until he reached the blockage. He found a piece of timber on the ground, and used it to prod the rubble near the roof.

He felt less resistance on the left side, and guessed that the roof had caved in from the right, filling the tunnel from that direction.

Carefully, he began to lift out pieces of rock near the top left corner, waiting a few seconds each time, listening for sounds of movement.

After removing half a dozen rocks, he shone his flashlight into the corner. As far forward as he could see, the ends of the roof beams were still attached to the vertical timbers on the left side, creating an archway skewed at forty-five degrees.

He worked in a horizontal position, squirming forward on his elbows, then backwards, pulling debris with him. Inch by inch he cleared a passage, roughly triangular in section, grading the base of the triangle to support the archway formed by the timbers.

Two hours later, he reached behind a piece of rock and felt a draft of air on his left hand. Cautiously, he pulled the rock towards him, then raised his head and shone the flashlight through the opening. The tunnel ahead was clear.

*   *   *

The tunnel continued about fifty yards beyond the blockage, and, as Wim expected, led to a winze, a shaft sunk from a point below surface. He shone his flashlight down the shaft and saw a rusty steel ladder sinking into the darkness. Still no electrical wiring or hoisting equipment.

He shook the frame of the ladder and gave it a strong push. It held. He slung the bag over his shoulder, adjusted his hard hat and stepped on to the top rung.

A hundred feet below, he reached a rudimentary station that was little more than a cave blasted out of the wall. No cross-cut or tunnel led from it. He decided to keep going.

He continued past the next station, and the next. Still no tunnels led off the shaft. At what he guessed to be the four-hundred-foot level, he stopped for a rest, then continued his descent.

The winze ended a hundred feet further down, connecting with a tunnel which sloped down from it at a slight gradient. This tunnel was larger, about twelve feet square. Again, no tracks, electrical conduit or air ducts.

Seventy yards down the tunnel, a flood-door blocked his path. The heavy steel door hung on timbers inset behind the rock, opening towards the other side. Wim decided that the original miners must have planned a series of egress tunnels, each to be equipped with such doors. If they hit an underground watercourse and could not control flooding in the main shaft, the men working on this side of the mine would not be trapped. They would reach the exit winze through tunnels above the flood level, and the winze itself would remain relatively dry.

Wim put his shoulder to the door, but felt no movement. He opened the bag, looking for a crowbar. They would not have used a hydraulic cylinder, he thought, but would have simply inset the door tightly, bracing it with barricades.

He could see that the door was hinged on his left, and began to work on the right side. He managed to dig the crowbar into the mid-point of the frame, and worked it in about six inches. Pulling with all his strength, he felt a barricade give slightly. He repeated the exercise at the top and bottom, then returned to the middle, and worked the three points successively until the door was ajar about two inches. Then he reached through the gap with the crowbar and levered the barricades upwards, out of their brackets.

Wim tried to push the door open, but still it resisted. Putting his back against it, he heaved, and the door moved an inch or two more. He was then able to get his foot in against the frame, and with this additional leverage managed to open the door two or three feet.

He shone his flashlight into the tunnel ahead, and saw what had been holding the door back. A pile of dried tailings mud, with the texture of coarse sand, topped with a thin, hard crust, was banked against the other side of the door. He took a step through the opening, and his flashlight caught an old-style miner's helmet, its Davey lamp still intact. There was a musty smell, with a hint of rotten eggs.

He put on his breathing mask, and as he did so his eye caught something else. Half-buried in the sand was a human skeleton.

He collected his bag and began to pick his way through the sand and silt, knee-deep in places, ankle-deep in others. Twice he stumbled over the bones of dead miners, and once he tripped, falling on his hands and elbows.

As he fell, he dropped his flashlight and his bag. He quickly raised himself on his hands, ready to move on, but then froze. The flashlight had landed an arm's length in front of him, and as he raised his head, he found himself staring directly at a skull caught in its beam. Shaken, he picked himself up and carried on.

The tunnel ended at a second winze fifty yards ahead. He decided to climb down it, but after twenty or thirty feet, the smell nauseated him, even through the mask, and he was slipping on the dried mud on the rungs of the ladder. He shone the flashlight downwards but could see nothing below. When he threw a piece of rock down the shaft, it disappeared without a sound.

He decided to follow the winze upwards. Counting the rungs, he stopped at the four-hundred-foot level, where he could see a timber walkway leading around the shaft to a station on the other side. He tested the planks before setting foot on them, then cautiously, his back against the wall, began to circle the shaft.

Almost immediately, a piece of timber gave way and fell into the void. Pressing himself against the wall behind him in shock, he almost dropped the flashlight. After a moment, he recovered, got down on his knees and checked the walkway closely. The planks, like the ladder, were covered with sediment, but otherwise felt firm and dry He suspected a dislodged support beneath the trestle, but reckoned the walkway would be safe if the other supports held. Continuing on his hands and knees, he inched his way round to the other side.

He came to a small station, an area of about fifty square feet, fenced off from the shaft. A tunnel leading up to the station had been widened at that point to create space for the station, which was fronted by wire mesh.

Double doors, eight feet high and four feet wide, also constructed of framed wire mesh, closed off the station. The doors were loose, and their hinges grated as he pried them open with his foot...

He sat at a dusty table inside, listening to the mine creaking around him in the darkness, and wondered what the plans had been for this shaft. He reached into his bag for a bottle of water, took a swig and put it back. He checked the time: twenty-five minutes to eleven.

After resting for a few minutes, he left the station and started along the tunnel, noting that it sloped upwards on this side. He was surprised to find that the tunnel ended less than fifty feet from the shaft, sealed by timber planks. He used his crowbar to pry a plank loose, and found rough concrete behind it.

He could not tell how old the concrete was, but thought it likely that the original miners had blocked off the shaft in order to close this side of the mine. He decided to check out the shaft above, to see if other tunnels had also been sealed.

He found tunnels at three hundred, two hundred and one hundred feet. In each case they had been sealed in exactly the same way as at four-hundred level. The winze ended at one hundred feet.

As far as he could see, the ceiling at one hundred feet was intact above both the tunnel and the winze, and he guessed that the cave-in had occurred just beyond the point where the tunnels were now sealed. The mud would then have gushed down one or more of the tunnels into the winze, flooding the winze and the escape tunnels on the other side.

He had seen enough. Under the weight of the tailings pond, a giant sink-hole had evidently opened up into the original mine, flooding at least one shaft and killing everyone in it. The owners had probably made an attempt to carry on after sealing the ingress points and the tunnels, but had then abandoned the mine before the weight of the tailings reached a dangerous level again.

Tailings were now being pumped into the pond at the rate of almost a hundred cubic yards every day, and the accumulated volume, allowing for natural seepage and evaporation, could be three or four hundred thousand cubic yards. In a few weeks, Wim thought, the rains would begin, adding to the weight.

It was now after five p.m. He decided to wait for nightfall before returning to Selya's cabin. In the meantime, he had some thinking to do.

He began to climb down the ladder, back to five hundred-level and the tunnel leading to the escape winze.

19

Stefan sat in front of Turr's desk, facing the window behind it, while Turr stood beside his desk, looking down at him. The angle made it hard for him to look directly at Turr, while at the same time he felt he was under a microscope.

Turr had made no sound except for an indistinct growl as he ushered Stefan into the room. He had directed Stefan to the chair with the back of his hand, and was now waiting for him to speak.

Stefan tried to breathe calmly and think clearly. Eventually, he said, "I have tried to contact the mine, but my colleagues are suspended, I think." He looked up at Turr, who continued to look at him as if expecting him to go on. "Can you tell me why I can not reach them?" he added after a pause.

There was a silence, then Turr said, "We can get information you need. I told you this."

"I would like..."

"Anita will get what you need." He reached for the phone. "Please excuse me."

Stefan was relieved that the meeting was over, despite the fact that his questions had not been answered. His first inclination was to get back to work, to avoid anything which might disrupt his pleasant life on the island. But he could not put the unanswered questions out of his mind. Why had Wim left the mine? Why had communications suddenly been suspended? And what type of sediment had Selya collected at twelve-hundred level? The more he thought about these questions, the more uneasy he felt.

20

Wim reached Selya's cabin shortly before eight in the evening. As arranged, she had left a rear window open, and the room was in darkness. He gave a short whistle to warn her before levering himself over the sill.

She gave him a beer, which he drank in a single draught, then sank back in his chair. She waited for him to speak, and when he was ready, he began to tell her what he had seen.

"So they must have tried to carry on," she said after he had finished.

"For a while. I think they sealed the tunnels at the point of the inrush, then continued to work the mine from the main shaft."

"But they must have known it was unstable."

"The deeper they went, the less chance the men could get out in time if there was a cave-in. And production costs would be rising as the depth increased."

"So now we know why they stopped at a thousand feet."

A thought struck him. "Or perhaps they were shut down."

"They would have been, if anybody had known about it."

"Can you get in touch with the ministry…"

"I'll make an appointment. They may let me go through the records."

They talked about the mine, changes in personnel, problems which had arisen and accidents which had happened. Todd Delahaye had found a position as mine captain in a South African mine, and would be leaving at the end of the month. Martin had taken over as mine manager. A man had fallen down the shaft, and had been found at the bottom missing a hand. They had looked everywhere for the hand, and Martin himself had spent some time with the crew assigned to search for it.

"One of the lashing crew finally found it, by accident," Selya told him.

"Where was it?"

"On the stage at seven-hundred level. He saw something which looked like a glove, a yellowish colour. He picked it up, then dropped it as if he'd picked up a scorpion."

"He must have grabbed the stage when he was falling," Wim said, thinking of the dead man. He remembered how close he had come to losing his footing himself, earlier in the day.

"You can't go back into the mine." She reached out and touched his hand.

He nodded. "I can stay at the farm tonight, if you drive me there," he said. "Then I'll see if Tony Tomlin will let me hide out at his place. He has the farm next to mine."

"They may be looking for you there."

"At the farm? They would probably go out during the day. I'll be safe for a few hours tonight."

They drove south, past Lusaka, towards Victoria Falls, then west thirty miles, reaching the empty farmhouse close to midnight. She leaned over and kissed him before he got out of the car, then quickly left. He stood outside for a few minutes, listening, then went round to the back of the farmhouse and let himself in quietly.

He lit a Tilley lamp, and sat looking at the shadows flickering and undulating over the corrugated iron roof and the wattle poles supporting it. As a boy, he had watched those shadows as his mother moved around the room, aware of the sweet scent of his father's tobacco and the comforting drone of their voices as he drifted off to sleep. But the room, once a place of warmth and security, was now cold and unwelcoming. Eventually, he fell into a shallow and restless sleep.

21

One arm over the seat back, Detective-Sergeant Ola hummed to himself in the front of an unmarked Land Rover. He held his head back in the attitude of a general returning from a successful campaign, so that the flesh bulged in folds at the back of his neck, which was wider than his head.

A black police van followed the Land Rover, a second Land Rover bringing up the rear. Two men, one of them missing an ear, rode in the back seat.

The convoy drove past the State House and turned into the grounds of a mansion, whose deep red brickwork clashed with bright yellow paintwork on its windows and doors. A sign on the guardhouse at the entrance read,

Department of Medical Research

NO ENTRY

Beside the house was a single-storey concrete building with a flat roof, about sixty feet square, its grey paint faded and peeling. Neither building showed signs of being occupied.

The vehicles drove between the buildings, turned right, and stopped. The occupants of the Land Rovers got out, and two of the men opened the rear doors of the police van while the others stood and watched.

A prisoner, flanked on either side by uniformed officers, his face luminous in the way a wanted man's face stands out in a crowd, sat inside against the partition, his hands handcuffed behind his back. As the spectators watched, one of the officers placed a paper bag over the man's head, then forced him to his knees in the van. The officers then got out, dragging the man between them.

Ola spoke to the officers, who left in the police van. The others then took the prisoner down a flight of steps and into the building.

22

Paxton saw the man crossing the lobby as he came down the stairs. Tall, white, about thirty-five, the man was moving in the general direction of the security desk.

Training and instinct put Paxton on the alert. Without changing pace or direction, and without looking up, he had come within six feet of the man when he saw the sudden contortion he was expecting.

Paxton was carrying his briefcase, which was made of lightweight metal, in his right hand, but in readiness had turned it slightly towards his left. Bringing his left hand under it, he swung it violently into the man's face, then, as the man tried to ward it off, wrestled his left arm behind his back and forced him to his knees. The briefcase had fallen to the floor but had not opened.

The manoeuvre was executed so swiftly and cleanly that the security guard had barely time to get out of his chair. Without taking his eyes off the man, Paxton told the guard to call for one of the detectives in the general office. "Get Tom to come down, please," he said.

The detective who responded handcuffed and searched the man, finding a South African passport, a wallet and car keys with a tag showing the make, model and licence number. Paxton glanced through the passport and wallet and scrutinized the key tag. Then he picked up his briefcase and led the way to the stairs leading to the floor below.

At the end of a corridor, past a storage area, was a row of interrogation rooms, each about ten feet square, windowless and furnished only with a table and two chairs. The walls of each room were painted cream above shoulder level, olive green below. They entered the first room.

In a business like tone, Paxton told the man to sit, then turned to the detective and said, "Find out what that was about, Tom. I'm off now." He walked towards the door.

The man said, "I will speak to you, Mr. Paxton. Nobody else."

Paxton had a choice. He could leave the man to Tom's mercies as a lesson for his arrogance, but if there was something personal behind the attack, he wanted to know about it.

To make the most of his advantage, he continued towards the door, his only response a slight raise of the eyebrows. As he opened the door the man spoke again, more urgently.

"I am asking you man to man."

Paxton turned to face him. He glanced at Tom Marutu. The detective was leaning against the wall, looking like a street gang leader in low-slung pants and T-shirt.

He took his time before replying, to keep up the pressure. Then he turned to the detective. "All right, Tom," he said. "I'll ring if I need you."

Marutu moved slowly and ominously past the suspect, stone-faced, communicating a readiness to act without mercy if given the word. As he was leaving the room, Paxton said to the man, "I have five minutes. Speak now." He sat down across the table as Marutu closed the door behind him.

"My name is Jan Kleikampp," the man said. "I served in the South African army for seven years, then in an anti-subversion unit…"

"You were in B.O.S.S.?"

"Yes."

"Go on."

"Since then, I have worked as a consultant in Angola, Burundi and Botswana."

"A mercenary."

Kleikampp nodded. "Three weeks ago, I received an assignment through the agency…"

"Which is?"

"Strategic Alliance Group—Capetown."

"Run by…"

"Anthony Hadler."

Paxton gave a flicker of recognition. An army officer like himself, Hadler had crossed the border in the seventies, contemptuous of people like Paxton who had allied themselves with the new regime.

"That explains who you are," he told Kleikampp. "Now tell me what you were told to do."

"My orders were to get your briefcase, Mr. Paxton. I was to fly here, hire a car, come to the State House, be in the lobby at about five-thirty and catch you when you were leaving for the day."

"What was supposed to be in the case?"

"I was given no information about that."

"What were you to do then?"

"I was to park with an empty space on my left. Someone would park next to me. When I came out they would be waiting to take the case. I would get into my car and leave."

"How were you going to get away?"

"I thought you would be out of shape. I saw some photographs. I thought I would be out of the door before you could react." He added that a van had parked next to him as he was getting out of his car, but he had avoided looking directly at it, and had not seen the driver.

"How do you think your contact recognized you?" Paxton asked him.

"He would recognize a hire car from the airport, and would have had a description of me."

"Did you book the car from Capetown?"

"No."

"How did you know there would be a car available at the airport?"

"I've been here before. There are always cars available."

"They have your credit card number on record, then."

"No, they accept cash. I paid the waiver and security deposit."

Paxton pondered whether someone with a military background would arrive at the airport without having arranged transportation in advance, especially when a schedule had to be met. On the other hand, to book in advance would have created an unnecessary record, and it was true that a car would normally be available at the airport. It was also likely that his contacts would have a description of Kleikampp, and may even have tailed him from the airport.

Whether or not Kleikampp's story was true, Paxton knew instinctively what his clients wanted.

His investigation of the missing Treasury funds case had led to a holding company which controlled the Cardinal Copper Wire Company, where he suspected the missing funds had been funnelled. One of the principals of the holding company had turned out to be David Mukuba, a businessman who owned the airport catering concession, and who also happened to be a son-in-law of Virgil Mpetu.

So far, Paxton had found no incriminating transfers or deposits, and in view of Mukuba's connections he was proceeding cautiously.

His office file contained only innocuous reports from staff. Any sensitive information was stored on a diskette, which he kept in a pocket in the briefcase.

He decided that someone had gone through the office file, and possibly his desk. They suspected he had more, and his briefcase was the obvious place.

He checked the time. Half an hour had passed since the skirmish in the lobby. He walked behind Kleikampp and picked up the briefcase. Then he turned to Kleikampp and said, "Stay where you are." He left the room, locking the door behind him.

He walked past the other interrogation rooms to a steel door at the end of the corridor. The door opened into a long passageway which curved to the left, its walls painted in the same colours as the interrogation rooms, its concrete floor painted grey. A hundred yards further, he opened another door into a corridor which led past rooms which looked like school laboratories, with long wooden tables equipped with bunsen burners, and wooden counters around the perimeter fitted with sinks. Hearing the sound of voices in one of the rooms, he stopped to listen for a minute, then continued along the corridor, through a door to his right and up a flight of steps into the open air.

He walked round the side of the Department of Medical Research, stopping for a moment to speak to the guard on duty. He turned left at the road and walked fifty yards to the entrance to the State House car park.

There were only about twenty cars in the lot, and he immediately spotted Kleikampp's car and the van on the front row, about fifty yards ahead of him. He crossed to the right side of the lot, then moved forward, keeping well to the right of the van, out of range of its rear-view mirrors.

As he came closer, he saw that the driver was sitting at the wheel, and judged from his attitude that he was alone. The engine was not running. He set the briefcase on the ground on the right side of Kleikampp's car and drew his gun.

He walked quickly around to the van and thrust the barrel through the open window against the driver's cheekbone, stepping quickly to the front of the door in case the man tried to slam it into him. In a clear, commanding voice, he told him to put his hands on this head, and as the man did so, he reached inside and took the keys out of the ignition. Then he drew back slightly, opened the door and told the driver to get out slowly, leaving his hands on his head.

He frisked the man, keeping his gun pointed at him, then took out his I.D. and held it up. "You know who I am," he said, in the same commanding tone.

The man remained silent, avoiding Paxton's gaze.

"Now I want to know who you are," he continued. He took out his cell phone. "You can tell me here, or we can go inside."

The man, a scruffy, bony-faced individual, began to look ill. In a high, wheezing voice, he said, "I am here for a delivery of a package."

"Where is the package?"

"Somebody going to bring it out here. I am waiting."

"And where are you going to take the package?"

The driver's eyes clouded, and there was a momentary hesitation until Paxton cocked his gun again. Then he said, " I will take it to the police station."

"Who are you going to give it to at the station?"

"I have to ask for the Chief Inspector."

"Who asked you to deliver the package?"

"Malcolm Ngebele. He is my boss."

Ngebele's cartage and delivery vehicles were a common sight in Lusaka.

Paxton had heard enough. He put his gun away, took out a card from his wallet and gave it to the man. "Go to the station and give this to the Chief Inspector," he told him. "Tell him there is no package today." He handed back the keys, then walked around Kleikampp's car and collected his briefcase.

He would take care of Tibuluma in due course, he thought. In the meantime, he would keep the slob guessing.

Instead of heading across to the reserved parking at the front of the building, he went back inside, across the lobby and down the stairs. Passing the interrogation rooms without pausing, he made for the passageway leading to the Department of Medical Research.

<h1 style="text-align:center">23</h1>

Paxton passed the laboratories, then tried the door of the next room, whose glass was covered on the inside by a blind. The door was locked, but he used a master key to open it, stepped inside and turned on the light.

There was a dentist's chair, a stretcher, an examination table, and a counter fitted with a sink and cabinets in the same way as in the adjoining rooms. Paxton smelled disinfectant, and noticed that the floor tiles were wet. He walked over to the counter and the examination table. They too were wet.

He went back into the corridor, leaving the door open, and walked along to a janitor's cupboard at the end. Inside were a number of bulging black garbage bags.

He pulled out the garbage bag which looked as if it had been the last to be thrown into the cupboard. Someone had spun the bag while holding the top until it formed a rope end, then tied a knot in it. He dug his nails into the knot and pried it open, then carefully opened the bag itself.

The smell hit him before he could focus his eyes on the contents. Glancing inside, he saw wads of blood-soaked brown paper towels before quickly spinning and knotting the bag as before. He threw it back on to the pile, closed the door, then returned to the open room to wash his hands at the sink. Then he retraced his steps through the passageway, left the State House through the lobby and got into his car.

As he drove out of the parking lot, he took out his cell phone and pressed the speed-dial code for the detectives' office. When Marutu came on the line he said, "Tom, I've left our assault suspect in the interrogation room. I'm not interested in charging him, but let him sit there for another hour before you let him go."

He then asked to speak to Ola, and was eventually patched through to Ola's car.

"Where are you?" Paxton asked him.

"On my way home, Bwana."

Paxton narrowed his eyes at the cooing, insolent tone. "You were in Medical Research this afternoon?" he asked curtly.

Ola made a humming sound which turned into the word "Yes."

"Why?"

There was another temporizing hum, then Ola said, "We had a suspect to question." The crooning tone told Paxton that Ola was smiling his radiant smile.

"In the Latonga case?" Paxton asked in disbelief.

"Yes, Bwana."

Paxton controlled himself with an effort. "Why was I not told?" he asked.

"Mmm…we were trying to soften him up first."

"So?"

"He was shot while trying to escape." Again, Paxton pictured Ola's exaggerated smile at the other end of the line.

"Who was he?"

"A man from the Kafue, Bwana. Somebody who fitted the description of the man who was hanging around after the shooting. You know we were going there yesterday with those two employees."

"I want a full report in the morning. I'll be in my office at seven." He switched off the phone, then swore at the top of his voice inside the car.

24

Six weeks after arriving in the Cayman Islands, Stefan was half-way through the first draft of his report. Turr was responding promptly to his requests for reports of shaft development, ore processed, costs and yields, profit and market trends, and Stefan found nothing inconsistent or implausible in the data provided. But questions continued to simmer in his mind.

A few days after he had gone up to Turr's office, he asked Turr whether he could spend a day on Grand Cayman.

"There is nothing to see there," Turr told him, his face inscrutable.

"I have a few things to buy."

"Anything you need, give your list to Aaron. He will take care of it."

Stefan had to agree that he wanted for nothing. When he had asked Anita to cut his hair, she had told him that he was already on the hairdresser's list, as well as the doctor's list, in case he ever needed medical attention. "You are on all the lists," she had said with a laugh, referring to the people who were constantly arriving by helicopter. He had no reason to leave the island, other than the thought that he might be able to call the mine from Grand

Cayman, since the telephones in the computer room and in his cottage handled internal calls only.

"Finish your work," Turr said, "you can go—anywhere you like."

Stefan returned to his desk, thinking that he might be able to finish the report in another three weeks. But the nagging doubts persisted.

Two days later, when Anita came down to collect an instalment, he asked her to contact the mine for some updated production data. Instead of taking a note back to her office to fax the mine, she sat down at a terminal, then called out to him to repeat the information he needed.

Stefan got up from his desk and went over to the computer room, answering as he did so. He took care to stand to one side of the terminal, to avoid appearing inquisitive, but as he looked down at her from that angle, her dark, lustrous hair falling against her slender arms, her exotic eyelashes downcast over the keyboard, he found her irresistably desirable.

She stood up as he came forward, her expression suddenly dream-like, her lips parted. He pulled her to him, and she gave a breathless cry, a soft, musical sound which took on an urgent note as they folded into each other's arms.

*   *   *

She smoothed her dress and hurried out, collecting the printed sheets on her way. As she left the room, she said, "Complete the message and PF3."

He sat at the terminal and looked at the unfinished message, which indicated "Destination: AHC524710" at the top of the screen. He had no idea whose code this was, but thought it might belong to Ulame or one of his team, since production data was being requested. He thought for a moment, checked his notes for his own code, then finished the original message and added:

"Please also provide analysis of recent samples at 1100 level by Selya Paxton. E-mail reply to EJC264587.

25

Martin put down the phone and turned to Selya. "The Ministry has no record of any mining here before we arrived two years ago," he said.

"So the records have been destroyed."

Martin raised his eyebrows and shrugged. "I have no idea," he said.

"But at least we have enough evidence to close the tailings pond. We can find another site."

"I'll need authorization from Mr. Turr."

"We can't afford to wait. Lives could be at stake."

"I can explain that to Mr. Turr."

Selya stood up to leave the office. She understood Martin. He was uncomfortable in his new role as Wim's successor, and afraid to do anything without Turr's blessing.

"Before you go," Martin said, "Stefan has just E-mailed, asking for your test results on the bore-hole debris."

"Can I see it?"

"Well, I was just going to reply that we have some information to discuss with Mr. Turr."

"I just want to say hello."

Martin hesitated, then turned to his terminal and brought up Stefan's message. "Actually, I can say hello for you when I write back," he said.

"Martin, I really would like to let Stefan know about Wim. Can I write a short note? You know I don't have access."

Again, Martin hesitated. "Just give me the figures—I'll add them to the other information he wants," he said after a moment. Then he added, "I'll say hello from both of us." He spoke in a direct, natural way, and the tone of his voice was pleasant. Despite her frustration, she felt no anger towards him.

"By the way," Martin added, his face elated now, "I was waiting to tell you—Morag and Sam have just been released. They'll be back tonight."

Selya cheered, and they both laughed. "Congratulations—how did you manage that?" she asked him.

"No, I can't take any of the credit for it. Apparently they were told they could leave about an hour ago. That was it—no explanation. Morag rang just now from the hotel lobby. I've sent Joe to collect them."

"I knew everything would turn out all right."

"So now we're short only one."

"Chaku? There's no word about him?"

"Disappeared into thin air. The DNS were here looking for him on Tuesday, as you know, but he wasn't here."

"He'd worked the night shift."

"Yes."

"So he may have gone to his village, and they may have found him there."

"I rang the DNS, but they said they had nobody in custody by that name."

"We could check with his people."

"I will, but if he went there, there's no reason he wouldn't have got back here for his next shift."

They looked at each other, both unwilling to say what they were thinking: that they might not see Chaku again.

Selya remembered the information Stefan wanted. "I'll be back in a few minutes," she said, leaving the office.

Back at her desk, she took out the report and keyed a short note with the heading: "Debris/extrusion analysis". She printed the note, and was on her way back to Martin's office when she saw him running towards the shaft. "There's been an accident," he called out to her. "Call First Aid."

At the twelve-fifty level, the Lashing Shaft Foreman led him sixty or seventy yards along the cross-cut to an ore pass, a vertical bore hole about four feet wide. There were men at the edge with lanterns, and looking down, he could make out a red hard hat about a hundred feet below.

"Give me the chain," Martin said, pointing to a winch on the back of an electric cart. Grasping the chain and standing on the hook, he was lowered down to the injured man.

The man was in a sitting position, blood spurting from a finger-sized hole in the middle of his back, his torso twisted at over ninety degrees from his legs. He was moaning incoherently. There was no room to manoeuvre, and Martin had himself winched back up.

A doctor who came to the mine once a week was on hand, and by the time he arrived the men had hooked a small bucket to the chain. They winched him down, Martin hanging on to the chain above him.

The doctor examined the victim, then took out a syringe and injected him with morphine. "Let's go back up," he told Martin. At the top, he said quietly, "Just hook him under the armpits."

They did so, and by the time he reached the top of the hole, the man was dead.

An hour later, still unsettled, Martin went to Selya's office and told her what had happened, finding some refuge from his anguish in the beauty of her eyes.

She gave him the note she had written for Stefan. She had gone to his office after he had been called out, but had found his terminal locked. Now she had to hope that Martin would copy and send the note as written, and that Stefan would recognize its message.

26

A week had passed, and there had been no word from Stefan. Despite Turr's reputation as a difficult man to communicate with, Selya hesitated to by-pass him by contacting the Mines Department herself. She decided to speak to Martin again.

Martin saw her through the glass walls of his office, and waved her in. Before she could speak, he said, "I've spoken to Mr. Turr. He's coming here tomorrow."

"What did you tell him?"

"Just that you were concerned about the tailings pond."

"Did you tell him what Wim had found in the old shaft?"

"I said he had gone in there."

When Turr landed the next day, Martin was waiting at the airstrip. Turr was not alone: with him was a grey-haired man who got out of the Cessna holding a briefcase. Turr introduced him as John Thacker of the Mining Engineer's office.

They drove to the minehead, where Martin introduced Selya, who was waiting in his office. It was the first time she and Turr had met, and she was slightly in awe.

Turr wasted no time. "I am geologist also," he told her in the heavy accent she recognized as Russian, "and I understand how this…worries you." He wrinkled his eyebrows slightly to convey comradeship.

"Mr. Thacker has information which he will show you," he continued. "This will help you to understand." He glanced towards Thacker, who opened his briefcase and took out a brown envelope containing an assortment of plans, which he unfolded on Martin's desk.

Thacker's spoke in a muffled tenor. "These plans were submitted on behalf of Mr. Turr prior to operating the mine two years ago," he said. "They show the original shaft, the estimated position of the secondary shafts and the placement of the tailings dam." He paused while the others examined the drawings.

"Where did the information about the secondary shafts come from?" Selya asked.

Thacker looked at Turr, who said with a hint of impatience, "I have information, from the previous owner." Before Selya could speak, he added, "What is important, Mr. Thacker will now explain."

With an air of having endured an unnecessary interruption, Thacker pulled out another sheet and continued. "This is a survey indicating the gradient between the minehead and the south end of the tailings dam at six degrees from horizontal." He paused again while Martin and Selya looked over the plan.

"The plans indicate that the tunnels immediately below the tailings dam run parallel with the grade above," Thacker continued. "So they are also slanted away from the main shaft. In the event of a cave-in, tailings would therefore be channelled away from the main shaft."

Selya met Turr's eyes for an instant. He was watching her closely, his face set in a patient expression. She felt pressure to acquiesce now, while his patience held.

"However," Thacker continued, "we have no reason to expect a cave-in in the present situation, since the areas involved in the previous failure have evidently been filled and sealed, by previous operators."

Thacker's analysis seemed to correspond with Wim's report of the old workings, but Selya was not satisfied. "But if a cave-in did occur on this side," she insisted, "the mud would have nowhere to go but into the main shaft."

Thacker opened his mouth and lifted his hand as she spoke, to indicate that he had the answer to Selya's concern. "I'm not quite finished." He slid another drawing out of the sheaf.

"The present tailings dam is centered here." Thacker indicated a point on the diagram, and ran his thumb-nail vertically down the page. "If you dropped a plumb-line from here you would hit a point approximately seventy yards on the other side of the closure, and forty feet east of the mine workings.

"In the original mine, I calculate the centre—and the critical load point—to have been here, more or less directly above the sealed shaft area where the failure appears to have occurred. At this stage in the evolution of the dam, the dam is now centred beyond the mine, so that the risk of failure no longer exists." Still staring at the plans on the desk, he opened his eyes wide and blinked, waiting for a reaction.

"Do you mind if I look at the survey data?" Selya asked. Thacker again looked at Turr, whose expression did not change.

"Please. Take time," Turr said after a moment.

"I'd like to check the measurements. I think we all need to feel absolutely sure."

There was a pause, then Turr nodded to Thacker, who folded the plans, put them back into the envelope and handed it to Selya. "Review, please, in two days, and return this to Mr Thacker," Turr's tone implied extreme patience and self-control.

Neither Turr nor Thacker asked to go below surface or to meet any of the personnel, and after a brief conversation with Martin, they were driven back to the airstrip. Selya returned to her office and began to study the plans.

27

From the verandah of the Tomlin farmhouse, Wim watched the first rays of sunlight splintering through the wattle trees on the horizon, and felt the last desolate breath of night air on his face and arms. Presently, the rays coalesced, colours became distinguishable and the rich earth began to release its aroma. Grass birds, invisible within their cover, began to chirp and trill, and he could hear the screeching of primates resonating through the trees behind him.

Tomlin came out of the house as Wim was getting to his feet, and they exchanged subdued greetings. Tomlin lit a pipe, and they stood for a while gazing across the garden, through the trees into a small corn plantation beyond. Eventually, Tomlin straightened up and tapped his pipe on the railing. "Better get moving," he said, then added, "You've been up long?"

"Most of the night."

"Made any decisions?"

"I've decided to go to S.A. There's nothing I can do here to clear my name."

"Safer." He was an older man, short of breath.

They left the farm a hour later in Tomlin's Land Rover. As they reached the highway, Tomlin asked, "Straight to the airport?"

"No—I need a tax certificate first."

"I didn't realize that."

"To leave the country."

"The last time I was out of the country must be...thirty..." Tomlin's voice tailed off as he tried to calculate the years.

They reached the tax office shortly after nine thirty. Tomlin waited outside in the Land Rover. Wim took a number and sat at the back of the room near a cluster of people until his turn came twenty minutes later.

The woman behind the counter began to make out a receipt without taking her eyes off the form. "Passport, please," she said without looking up.

"I don't have it with me," Wim told her quickly, preparing to go out to the Land Rover to find it if necessary.

"Can you remember the number?" she asked. Again she did not look up.

In the heat of the moment, he was no longer sure of the number, but decided to take a chance. Any delay might draw attention to himself. "SR98824," he said.

The woman completed and stamped the receipt. "You are owing nothing." She pushed the receipt towards him. He thanked her and turned quickly away.

Back in the Land Rover, he found his passport in his carry-on bag and checked the number. "Thank God for that," he told Tomlin. "I've given them the right number."

They drove to the airport and stopped before entering the parking lot. Wim got out and lifted his luggage out of the back. "Don't wait," he told Tomlin. "I'll be in touch from S.A.."

"Can I pass on any messages to your friends?"

"Thanks, but it's best if there is nothing to connect you with me. I can let them know where I am."

Tomlin put the Land Rover in gear. "God bless," he shouted as he drove away.

Wim raised his hand in salute, then picked up his suitcase and bag and began to walk towards the terminal.

*   *   *

It was a quarter past eleven when he reached the South African Airways counter. "Return to Jo'burg," he told the attendant, giving her his passport and tax certificate.

"The next flight is at one o'clock." She glanced up at Wim, who nodded. Checking his suitcase, she completed the booking and returned his papers together with his boarding pass. "Your flight leaves from Gate Five, boarding at twelve forty-five," she said. "Have a pleasant flight."

He had over an hour to kill, and there was a bar on the departure level. He picked up his carry-on bag and headed for the escalator, stopping to buy a copy of the *Johannesburg Times* at a newsagent and boutique.

As he reached the escalator, a man approached from the opposite direction, also apparently heading for the departure level. They reached the escalator at the same time. The man stepped aside and courteously motioned to Wim to go ahead.

Wim felt his heart had stopped. The man was Colonel Ben Paxton.

28

The day after his visit to Empendwe, Turr called Chamberlain in Toronto. "There is something I like you to do." As usual, he neglected to introduce himself. His voice sounded detached, as though he were reading aloud to himself.

Chamberlain glanced out over the lake, bleached by pale winter sunlight filtering through the clouds. His eye caught a heavily-muffled jogger on his right, turning to retrace her steps along the deserted boardwalk. A pang of anxiety shot through his side, but he managed an enthusiastic greeting.

"My assistant, Kristiansson," Turr continued, "—he will finish our report, two weeks. Then, I think he does not go back to the mine. I like you to find him work in your company, until our project is finished. Your company can use engineer, I think."

Chamberlain swallowed. "Surely he can't work here without proper immigrant status." He struggled to find an obstacle. Kristiansson was too close to Turr. If he brought the man into the company, Chamberlain thought, it would advertise his connection with Turr.

"He is not immigrant," Turr replied. "He is employee of one of my companies, which has office in Canada. I send him for six months, he needs visa, which I have arranged already."

"But we can't be seen to have any connection, while…"

"Connection can not be made. The company is a numbered company, which is very difficult to trace to me."

"But he will be asked who he has been working for. Your name will…"

"He has been working for mining contractor, ReExploration. This also is very difficult to trace to me. And he will not mention my name."

Chamberlain fought to think clearly. He felt uneasy, but knew Turr was ready with an answer to all his objections.

"And of course, you will know not to put him in the same office which handles our claim," Turr added.

"When is he arriving?" Chamberlain asked weakly.

"He will telephone from his hotel. Two weeks, three weeks."

Chamberlain felt a dull ache in the pit of his stomach as he put down the phone. He felt trapped. By using his influence to arrange employment for Kristiansson at Imperial Platinum, he would be marking himself as Turr's man. If anything went wrong with the claim, the investigation would inevitably lead to him, and he would be exposed as an accomplice.

Now he was beginning to understand. There was more to it than simply keeping this Kristiansson under wraps until the claim had run its course. This was Turr's way of motivating him to make sure nothing did go wrong.

But Kristiansson's time at Imperial Platinum need not be a bed of roses, Chamberlain thought. He would make the young man welcome and help him to blend in as inconspicuously as possible, and Turr would have no reason to complain. But once the claim had been paid, Kristiansson had to go, and go quickly. Even back in Ireland, under a new name, he would sleep more soundly if Kristiansson were at a safe distance from Imperial Platinum, where his presence might prompt questions—questions that might lead to an investigation, perhaps by Interpol. Chamberlain's paranoia began to rise like a fever.

As he lay awake that night, Chamberlain realized that when the time came, Turr could not be relied upon to recall Kristiansson from Toronto. Once he had his money, Turr would have no further interest in the mine or his former employees. He would simply leave Kristiansson to his own devices, and as likely as not, Kristiansson would decide to stay in Toronto. As a prospective immigrant, he had more than enough education and work-experience to qualify; and if Kristiansson had a choice, surely he would rather sit in an office in a civilized country than risk life and limb in a mine, somewhere in darkest Africa.

Chamberlain realized it would be up to him to find a way to remove Kristiansson from Imperial Platinum when the claim had come to fruition. He began to identify his options.

The ideal solution would be to have the man killed, but he had no experience with that sort of thing. To fire him on some specious pretext—an area in which he did have experience—might create personal enmity. Kristiansson might start thinking, he might start talking, questions might be asked, giving rise to the investigation Chamberlain desperately wanted to avoid.

In any event, Chamberlain thought, he and Kristiansson should not leave the company at the same time. The connection between them should be minimized as far as possible.

He decided on an indirect approach. He would be a benevolent mentor to Kristiansson, who would then have nothing to complain about on his account, and there would be no scores to settle later. But Kristiansson's life could be made difficult in other ways, and the stage could be set for his demise in due course, once his mentor had departed.

There was a man in the General Division, Gavin Grince, a man whose career had been distinguished by the alienation of fellow-employees he had been appointed to manage. During his twenty years in the company, his seniors had considered removing him several times, but lacking evidence of anything "concrete", they had dissolved into indecision on each occasion. Chamberlain had never tried to conceal his distaste for Grince, and had gone so far as to tell people in the Select Risks Division that they should have no fear that Grince would ever be inflicted on them. But promises were made to be broken, especially when a personal agenda was at stake. The position of Special Risks Claims Manager was now open, and Grince was the man for the job, Chamberlain concluded.

29

At first glance, Stefan was disappointed that Selya's analysis, relayed to him by Martin, offered no comments or conclusions. The samples contained traces of copper and other elements, but nothing unusual. As far as Stefan could see, any random sample of rock might have yielded the same results. The message conveyed nothing significant.

Except for the word "extrusion".

He looked at the word, closed his eyes for a moment, then looked at it again. He had asked for the results of the analysis of the debris, so would have expected the reply simply to be headed, "Debris analysis". Martin, he was sure, would have had no reason to insert the incongruous word "extrusion". The terminology had to be Selya's. It had to be her way of confirming that the debris was tailings material—because only rock which had been processed and disposed of as tailings could be extruded or squeezed through an opening.

He picked up the telephone, called Turr's extension, and told Anita he needed to speak to Turr urgently. Twenty minutes later, she called him back to say that Turr was on his way down.

Turr entered the room and stood expectantly beside Stefan's desk. Unsure of himself, Stefan got to his feet and began to explain his concerns, but was interrupted almost immediately by Turr.

"This has been reviewed by government engineer. All plans and surveys have been explained to Miss Paxton. Tailings pond is now in different position from the old mine. Even if it had been in same position, that side of the mine is now closed."

"Could I see the documents?"

"I will telephone Mr. Thacker." Turr looked down at him, his face inscrutable. "He will speak to you and explain. You can discuss with him."

Stefan was slightly in awe of Thacker's authority, and was more than ready to defer to his expertise when they spoke by telephone in Turr's office the next day. He also felt that if the government mining authorities had investigated and were satisfied that there were no grounds for concern, the matter could be pursued no further in any event. He gave up any thought of asking to see the plans, and the fact that they had been lent to Selya was never mentioned.

He thanked Thacker for taking the time to telephone, and asked whether he should raise the issue in his report.

For the first time, Thacker hesitated. Then he said, "Our file has all the information we need, and we don't consider the placement of the pond a valid concern. However, if you feel you need to refer to our investigation in the course of your report, that is up to you. From our point of view, it's not necessary."

Stefan thanked Thacker again and handed the phone back to Turr, who waited until Stefan had left his office before speaking. "There is no problem," he told Thacker. "The report will say nothing about this."

"I've heard nothing from the girl."

"The papers will be returned tomorrow. I will make sure. She will have nothing to say." He stood up, grunted into the telephone and hung up.

30

When Turr told him he was being transferred to Toronto, Stefan had mixed feelings. He would miss the beauty and isolation of the island, and he would miss Anita, but he had known that his assignment there was temporary, and he was also beginning to feel ready to move on.

On the flight to Toronto, he found himself next to a young woman who began to make conversation as soon as the plane was airborne. She told him that she was a member of the Canadian Armed Forces, returning to base after a vacation.

"Do you see many countries?" he asked her.

"Only when I'm on vacation," she smiled.

She was petite, blonde, about twenty-five. "What kind of work are you assigned?" Stefan asked her.

"Communications." Her voice was bright and friendly, but she seemed wary of saying more.

"Do you work inside?" he asked, curious about life in the military.

"No—well, part of the time. The schedule varies."

"I know—there are always so many different things to do," he said.

Taking his comment as a reference to his own experience, she used it as an opening to ask him about his work.

He told her of his experience as a mining engineer and his recent assignment on the Cayman Islands, adding that he had been sent to Toronto to work for an insurance company.

"What will you do there?" she asked.

"I think it will involve claims to be paid," he said.

She looked at him and laughed heartily.

Stefan wondered what was so amusing, but hesitated to reveal his ignorance of the insurance world. "Well, I don't know how long I will be posted there," he said casually.

As the plane taxied to a halt and the passengers began to crowd the aisle, Stefan wished the young woman well and had started to get to his feet when she handed him a note. "You can reach me at this number," she said. "I'd like to know how things work out."

He made his way out of the plane, through the covered walkway and into the terminal. As he waited for his luggage at the carousel, he took out the note and read the name "Cpl. Annette Peters". Below the name was a telephone number.

He looked around, but did not see her. He folded the paper and put it in his wallet.

31

As he rode up the escalator, Wim felt the hair bristling on the back of his neck. There were people in front of him, and Paxton was right behind. The only way out would be to vault over the handrail and make a run down the other side. But there would be men at the exits.

At the top of the escalator, he walked slowly ahead, expecting to feel a hand on his shoulder at any moment. He passed through the security check, and continued towards the bar. Still no one approached him.

He ordered a brandy and Coke, knocked it back and ordered another. On his left, he heard Paxton say, "And the same for me."

Out of the corner of his eye, he saw that Paxton had taken a seat at the bar, three places away. Wim continued to stand.

Raising his eyes to catch the barman's attention, Wim signalled for a refill. As he did so, he glanced in the mirror behind the bar, then abruptly lowered his eyes. Between the glass shelves, between brightly coloured labels of Cinzano and Martini Rossi, he had caught sight of a uniformed officer. The man was at a table at the back of the room, facing the bar.

Wim finished his drink and left some money on the bar. "Back in a minute," he told the barman with a forced smile.

He headed for the washroom, his mind reeling. They were planning to arrest him as he boarded the plane, he thought. That would make more of an impact on the front pages. The washroom had no windows, and no other exits. He splashed cold water on his face, trying to clear his mind. After a minute, he straightened up slowly, reached for the paper towels and dried his face and hands.

He had reached the door when it opened suddenly from the other side, forcing him to step back smartly. To his horror, he found himself face to face with Paxton. But their eyes did not meet, and Paxton brushed past him without any sign of recognition.

He checked the time. There was still about half an hour before boarding. He went back to the bar. Through the mirror, he could see the uniformed officer, still in his position at the back of the room.

Paxton returned, and without a word spoken, was served by the barman. The minutes passed, and the two men kept pace with each other, neither acknowledging the other, neither showing any signs of impairment.

When the pre-boarding announcement came, Wim stiffened. Now it was a matter of minutes before general boarding.

Paxton had already left the bar, and was being checked through the gate. He would be waiting at the steps, Wim thought. The officer waiting at the back would bring up the rear guard.

After a minute, the stewardess announced business-class, and then general boarding. Mechanically, Wim paid the barman and moved towards the gate. The officer got up from his seat and began to move forward.

The gate opened on to stairs leading down to the tarmac. With about twenty other passengers, Wim went out into the searing heat, towards the waiting plane.

Apart from the other passengers, the only person he could see on the tarmac was a baggage handler. So they must be waiting for him on board.

He reached the plane, climbed the steps and went inside. A stewardess pointed him towards his seat.

Paxton's bull-like head caught his attention as soon as he entered the first-class section. But Paxton was alone, occupying a seat on Wim's left. There were no officers in sight.

Wim found his seat, and waited. Perhaps Paxton was waiting for back-up, he thought.

Eventually, he heard the door close, and the turbines began to whine. The plane backed away from the gate and began to taxi towards the strip. The stewardesses demonstrated safety procedures and checked seatbelts and cabin luggage.

The plane reached the take-off strip and stopped, waiting for clearance. Three, four minutes passed, and Wim began to feel uneasy. Perhaps the back-up had arrived. There was still time to call the plane back to the gate.

Then the engines roared into action, the plane hurtled forward and tilted upwards. He took a deep breath and closed his eyes as the plane soared into the clouds.

Minutes later, he heard a voice and looked up to see Paxton leaning over the seat beside him. "Mr. Van Dyk," he was saying. "May I have a word?"

Wim tried to stay calm. He nodded, and Paxton squeezed into the vacant seat.

"I couldn't say anything at the airport," he said brusquely. "There was no sense in attracting attention, with one of my men there."

Wim thanked him warily, trying to read his expression.

Paxton glanced around. There was an elderly couple in the row behind them; no-one immediately in front. "I think we can help each other." Paxton turned to face Wim, looking directly into his eyes.

"How can I...?!"

"This is a small country," Paxton began. "Everybody knows me, and it's my job to know everybody else. It's part of my job to investigate people."

"I investigated the people involved in your mining venture, including yourself. It was purely routine, but I saw qualities I liked, and I've kept you in my sights."

He glanced around again, then leaned towards Wim. "A situation has developed," he continued, "which I can't handle through normal channels. I need an outsider—an outsider with your background."

"What exactly…?"

"Money has been siphoned out of the Treasury, possibly invested in legitimate businesses. There appears to be a connection with the copper industry." He looked pointedly at Wim. "You will be liaising with contacts abroad, developing information, using your mining background as a cover. You will be given specific instructions." He paused, then added, "If you can help me, I may be able to clear your name in the Latonga affair."

Even before Paxton had finished speaking, Wim was ready to accept. He felt an intuitive respect for Paxton, who was treating him as a free agent, when he could have applied pressure ruthlessly. He also appreciated the risk Paxton must have taken in helping him to escape. The offer to help him clear his name—and ultimately return home—settled the question.

"What would you like me to do?" he asked.

"This contains the name and telephone number of your principal contact," Paxton reached for his wallet and took out an envelope, "and an advance. I want you to get on the next available flight to London, and call him when you arrive. He will brief you and give you directions."

Wim glanced into the envelope and saw a sheaf of banknotes and a slip of paper. He dropped it into his bag, then said, "I appreciate your help, Mr. Paxton. Can I make one other request?"

"Yes?"

"I was looking into a potential problem at the mine when I had to leave. There had been a cave-in under the tailings pond some years ago..."

"I know something about it. Selya came to see me when she was returning some survey documents. The ministry were giving her some kind of flim-flam—which didn't surprise me."

"I still feel responsible for the mine..."

"I understand." Paxton held up his hand. "But nobody is going to overrule the Mining Engineer. To ask the Acting Minister to intervene would be a complete waste of time," he added with an expression of disgust.

"A survey could be done by an independent engineering firm from S.A."

"You would have to cast enough doubt on the Mining Engineer's findings to justify engaging other experts. Again, the Acting Minister would have to intervene, and the way things are, that isn't going to happen."

Wim shook his head in frustration, but he understood the situation. He thought of Selya, and as if reading his mind, Paxton added, almost to himself, "I want Selya out of there—out of the country if possible."

Before Wim could pursue the subject, Paxton clapped his hands on the arms of his seat and began to get up. "I should get back," he said. "When we get off the plane, act as if we have never met. All right?"

Wim nodded as Paxton heaved himself to his feet. He watched the big man lumber down the aisle back to the front of the plane, then reached for his carry-on bag and took out the envelope. After making sure that nobody could see him, he counted ten thousand rand and two thousand pounds sterling. Then he read the name and telephone number written on the slip of paper. The name, which meant nothing to him, was Geoffrey Arnald.

32

An hour after landing at Pearson, Stefan was hurtling towards downtown Toronto in the comfort of an airport limousine, marvelling at the vastness of the expressway, which seemed at least a quarter of a mile wide, with a dozen lanes of vehicles screaming over the concrete in each direction. Here and there, he could see the roofs of houses nestling below the hotel and apartment towers dominating the skyline, and wondered how people could lead stable lives in such a turbulent and transient environment. But soon a serene expanse of lake, bordered by trees and parks, appeared on his right, and on his left an arresting view of the CN Tower and the skyscrapers in the heart of the city, walls of glass reflecting the golden glow of the evening sun.

The next morning, he left his hotel near the waterfront and walked up to the financial district. The offices of the Imperial Platinum Insurance Company were in a squat building clad in brown marble, dwarfed by the skyscrapers surrounding it. In the lobby, he spoke to a young man seated behind a counter. The man made a telephone call, then told him that Chamberlain would be right down.

While he was waiting, Stefan glanced round the lobby and saw a display case containing what appeared to be memorabilia of the company's past. There were antique pens, insurance contracts dating from the nineteenth century, and shields and insignia of a dozen insurance companies. A banner on the wall read, "We Appreciate You", and beside it, a framed manifesto proclaimed "Our Three Principles". He moved nearer the display, intending to read the smaller print underneath the heading.

"These were companies which were taken over by Imperial Platinum over the years," he heard a voice say. He turned to see a middle-aged man with thinning grey hair standing behind him.

"You must be Kristiansson," the man continued breathily. "I'm Fraser Chamberlain, Vice-President, General Insurance and Claims. I see you found us from my directions all right." They shook hands, and Chamberlain led the way along a winding corridor, then through double doors into another corridor flanked by numbered meeting rooms.

"So take-overs are quite common in your business?" Stefan asked as Chamberlain opened one of the doors.

"Oh yes, it's been going on for a hundred, two hundred years. Sometimes the older companies are forgotten, but they're still part of our history."

"And you can trace your ancestry back to those companies," Stefan smiled.

Chamberlain looked sharply at him, then smiled back warily. "We pride ourselves on Moving Forward here," he said. "But a historic image is important too."

He offered Stefan coffee from a tray, and they sat facing each other across the table.

"I've arranged for you to attend an induction session this morning," Chamberlain said. "We have them every fortnight, and it so happens you've arrived on the right day. But I wanted to see you as soon as you arrived." He gulped his coffee.

"Mr. Turr told me that he wanted you to get some insurance exposure," he continued, "and we're glad to have you here, because we can learn something from people like you. But Mr. Turr does want you to keep a low profile, as we say, and not mention that you've worked indirectly for him." He looked closely at Stefan.

"That is right. I can mention my work as a mining engineer, and mention the subsidiary contractors' names…"

"Yes. Mr. Turr is a policyholder, and some people might object to having an associate of his gaining inside knowledge, as it were…I don't feel that way myself, of course—I think we both benefit from having you here—but it's always wise to be careful." Chamberlain took another gulp of coffee, then set his cup down, turning it back and forth on the saucer to be sure it was properly positioned.

"Now," he continued, "a few other things. First of all, I think you need to move out of your hotel as soon as possible, for Mr. Turr's sake, and it might create some gossip if you were known to be living in a hotel. Here's the name of a rental agency—they'll find you an apartment in the range you feel you can afford, as close to the office as possible. I'll leave this to you."

"Thank you."

"Now I've arranged for you to work in our Select Risks Department, because they get involved in the areas where you would be most useful—mining, heavy equipment and such like. Also the professional liability claims—we have quite a high volume of those. Your background will be valuable in cases where engineers are being sued because a building has collapsed, where they have miscalculated the load, that type of thing. After your induction, I'll take you to meet the S.R.D. people. Just ask the front desk to give me a ring."

Stefan thanked him again.

"And the other thing was, I'd like you to report to me on anything important, or anything problematic. Especially on the professional liability claims. Of course we don't want anybody feeling that there are special relationships, of course—we're all part of a team— that's part of our culture. But at the same time, I have to report to the president, so I need to know everything that goes on, and the president and I also have to adjust the bulk reserves."

"Bulk reserves?" Stefan was mystified.

"Yes, on some classes of business it's more convenient to set aside a lump sum, as it were, rather than to try and estimate each claim separately." Seeing that Stefan was still puzzled, he added, "Of course we're required by the government to set aside what we think we're going to have to pay out in claims—so we generally post a figure—a reserve—against each claim. But as I say, on some types of claim we use bulk-reserving—for example, where we pay out over a number of years, say for an environmental cleanup, where we don't think we should have to reserve all our eventual payout right at the moment. So we don't post an individual reserve, we reserve a ball-park figure for the whole group of claims."

The vocabulary of insurance was new to Stefan, and he would have asked Chamberlain to elaborate, but he realized that for the moment, he was supposed to understand only the importance of the prescribed line of communication. He thanked Chamberlain for taking the time to meet him, and the vice-president showed him the way to the theatre, where the induction session was to be held.

There were about twenty people in the theatre. On the right side of a small stage, a young woman stood at a lectern, testing a video control panel. From time to time, disjointed patterns flashed on the screen behind, and after a few minutes, she leaned over the lectern to speak to a woman in the audience, who then joined her to help with the controls.

Finally, the lights were dimmed, and with a deafening crash of rock music, a montage of colourful images appeared on the screen: people conferring happily around a computer terminal, women golfing on a green, people nodding in agreement around a conference table, more outdoor shots, this time of blue seas and a yacht, then a spinning globe which came to a halt above New York, where the company's world headquarters zoomed into view. The cameras then cut to an interview with the president of the company, seated amiably on a sofa near his desk, which could be seen piled with documents.

"Imperial Platinum's success," the president was saying, "lies in our visionary leadership and our people—their knowledge, their experience, and their team spirit." We pick our people carefully, we develop them, and we mould them into a professional team which is second to none. And we operate on a level playing field where we're empowered, and where we can all get ahead based on merit and hard work. This is the Imperial Platinum culture.

"You can all be proud to be part of the Imperial Platinum culture, and part of a business which is like no other. I'm always amazed at how we in the insurance business have an insight into the whole spectrum of human activity. Whether it's manufacturing, or pipelines, automobiles or art collections, we cover it all. You could find yourself adjusting a claim on a painting by Van Gogh, or a Stradivarius violin, or you might be involved in underwriting a major project for one of the industrial giants, and you can think what a privilege it is to have an insight into all these walks of life."

"We are in business to give service—to give the best service in the industry—and to do that, we not only have to have the best team, we also have to have the best equipment. Our new computer system in Canada, for example, is costing ten million—maybe more, maybe twenty—I hope it isn't more than twenty—and we have a hundred and fifty people seconded from regular duties for two years, at a cost of another ten million, to adapt the system to our needs, so that the public gets the best service possible."

"The more they spend on computers, the more paper piles up," someone murmured next to Stefan.

Off-camera, the interviewer asked how the company was increasing its profile in the community.

"We have done surveys which indicate that most people know the name of their broker better than the name of their insurance company," the president said. "In fact, passers-by have been interviewed from the front steps of our building, who had never heard of Imperial Platinum."

"New ads are going to change that. We're going to project a more upbeat image, and we're going to get across the fact that we've been around for a long time. We can look back at almost two centuries of service, through the various companies in our stable, and at the same time we are a visionary, forward-moving organization, positioned for leadership in the global economy. So we've developed what I think is a catchy phrase: 'Moving forward for you for a hundred and fifty years'."

After answering a few more prepared questions, the president shifted in his seat, leaned forward and addressed the camera with a serious expression. "I've talked about our long history of service, our expertise, and our culture," he said. "Moving forward, I want these three principles to be enshrined in our consciousness, especially the people watching this who are new to the company. Service, Expertise, and Culture," he spoke in capitals. "These are the three pillars of our organization—the three principles of our existence. And the most important of these is our culture. That's what sets us apart from the others. We appreciate You. We take care of you."

The lights came on, and the young woman at the lectern invited the new recruits to pick up a copy of the company's benefits manual as they filed out. "We are scheduling presentations on the latest changes to the pension and medical benefits," she said. "Your leaders will let you know the dates."

33

The telephone purred at the other end of the line, the double rings muted and distant. Eventually, Wim heard a muffled voice.

"…Lodge."

"Sorry?"

"Whom would you like to speak with, sir?"

"Geoffrey Arnald, please."

"If you'll give me your number, sir, I'll ask him to ring you."

Half an hour later, Wim picked up the telephone as it rang.

"Van Dyk."

"Geoffrey Arnald." The cultured voice carried well, although the line was still faint.

"There's no need to introduce yourself," Arnald continued. "I've been expecting to hear from you. Are you alone?"

"Yes."

"Look, I think we should meet, but you'll have to come to me. Can you write this down?" He waited until Wim was ready, then began to dictate instructions, each word precise and melodious.

After breakfast the next morning, Wim took a taxi to Paddington Station. Two hours later, he was in Oxford, walking down The Broad towards Arnald's college.

Massive entrance gates led to a portico within the stone walls, beyond which Wim could see a great clock above a verdant expanse of grass. Beside a bulletin-covered wall on his left, Wim noted a low archway through which he thought he could see a small office. He bowed his head to pass under the archway and up two stone steps into the Porters' Lodge.

He was directed to the staircase Selya had climbed three years earlier, and at the third landing found Arnald waiting in his doorway. Without a word, the professor ushered him inside and closed the door.

Wim saw books and papers piled everywhere, on a table, on the chairs, in bookcases, on the window seats. Fascinated, he was surveying the room, and its view of the quadrangle below, when he felt the force of Arnald's raw, penetrating gaze.

Without the hint of a smile, Arnald motioned Wim to a chair. Then, in a surprisingly civil tone, he offered sherry. Slightly unsure of himself, Wim accepted. Arnald poured from a decanter, handed Wim a glass, then began filling his pipe.

After enquiring courteously about Wim's journey from Zambia and his hotel accommodation, Arnald began deftly to probe his background and character. The interview was so skilful that within twenty minutes, Wim felt that no aspect of his life had been left unexposed. In return, he asked Arnald how he came to be involved in the affairs of a foreign country.

"I've never been active in politics—except of course as a political scientist," Arnald puffed comfortably on his pipe, his eyes almost closed, "but I used to do intelligence work in my younger days, and over the years I've got to know a few people in the field. I suppose you could call me a consultant." He continued to puff without taking his eyes off Wim.

"Now about this assignment. I don't want you to think that this is an unusual situation. If anything, we prefer people who have no connection with government or politics." He drew on the pipe. "People who have established themselves in some other field."

"Why is that?"

"Several reasons." Arnold gave him a searching look. "You're much more convincing when you don't have to act a part. You can also concentrate on a particular aspect of an enquiry without being burdened with extraneous information. And of course it's less expensive to use people who are not pensionable employees."

"I'm not a trained investigator."

"We don't want you to be. Trained investigators tend to be rather obvious." He stood up to refill Wim's glass. "I find they're better used sparingly—for specific purposes, and only when necessary."

"Now Colonel Paxton is interested in the Cardinal Copper Wire Company," Arnold continued. "The information filed with the authorities tells us very little. We think you can find out more about this company and its principals in person, as a representative of the copper-mining industry."

"I'll be happy to do what I can."

"I'd like you to read this material"—Arnold leant over the arm of his chair and reached for a crumpled brown envelope—"and dispose of it before you leave London. Make sure that any notes you keep would be meaningless to anyone else."

"When would you like me to leave?"

"A package will be delivered to your hotel in London during the next day or two. It will contain business cards and credentials of the Zambian Export Development Association, a credit card, a driver's licence and membership in a last-minute air travel club, among other things. When you receive the package, book your flight to Toronto through the club."

"That should save a fair amount."

"It also fits your unobtrusive image. Don't throw money around unnecessarily."

Arnold stood up. "Now I do have a few things to do, and I have a tutorial at four. Unless it's urgent, please telephone only between six and six thirty in the evening, which is one to one thirty Toronto time. You'll be put through to me if you call then. But you can fax at any time."

Wim wound his way down the staircase, and when he reached the archway at the corner of the quadrangle, he took a moment to step into the garden on the other side. It was a pleasant Spring day, and he could see three or four students on the lawn beneath the tree and on the gravelled walkway circling the lawn. The garden was surrounded by a moist and fragrant border of plants and flowers, and by a high stone wall.

He turned away from the stillness and serenity of the garden, feeling that he did not belong there, eager to get on with his assignment. He retraced his steps along the edge of the quadrangle, past the Porters' Lodge and out into the street. Fifteen minutes later, he was standing on the platform at the railway station, waiting for the next train back to London.

34

As Stefan left the theatre with his glossy folder, he found himself shoulder-to-shoulder with three other men at the door. "Hi, I'm Don Gibson," one of them said cordially, giving a strong handshake.

Stefan introduced himself and shook hands with the others, aware of alert, watchful faces. The men were all slightly above average height, heavy-set.

"Time for a quick sandwich?" Don asked, looking at his watch. "Or do you have other plans?"

It was a quarter to twelve. "I don't have to see Mr. Chamberlain until one thirty," Stefan answered.

"Sure, we'll get you back before then." Don put his arm out behind Stefan, ushering him forward. "We have a car right here." He led the way to the stairway beside the elevator, then down a flight of steps to a parking level below.

"So parking space is available here?" Stefan asked as they climbed into a green minivan.

"This is a company car," Gibson told him. "We work outside most of the time."

"This is not your first day?"

"No, we've been aboard a few months. Jim and I started the same day, and Greg a week later. They hold these introductory sessions every two or three weeks or so, but this is the first we could attend."

They spiralled up a narrow concrete ramp and through an automatic overhead door leading to the street. After a few turns, they were below the elevated highway which Stefan had travelled the previous night. Don drove aggressively, apparently confident that other traffic would yield.

Five minutes later, they turned away from the lakeshore into a semi-industrial area, and wove through the streets until they reached a row of brick buildings facing overgrown railway tracks. On the corner, beside an Italian grocery and a body shop, was a tavern. They parked on a residential street around the corner and walked back.

Don led the way up a narrow flight of stairs, past a smoke-filled bar on the ground floor. Upstairs, they found a table in a long, open room with a bar at one side, and a large television screen at one end. The furniture was spartan, the carpeting threadbare.

Don exchanged greetings with patrons at two or three other tables, all of them middle-aged men who looked up, then resumed quiet conversations amongst themselves. The bartender unloaded a tray of small glasses of beer. "Four hot veal, gentlemen?" he asked, to general assent.

"So where're you from, Stefan?" Don asked as they sampled spiced olives which Greg had bought from the corner store. Stefan gave them a brief résumé of his career, then asked the others the same question.

"We're all from Canada," Don said. "I'm from Toronto, Jim's from B.C., and Greg's from Toronto as well. We're all ex-police officers, we've all worked for the Insurance Crime Prevention Bureau, and now we're part of the Special Investigation Unit at the I. P."

"Actually, I have never worked for an insurance company," Stefan admitted. "I don't know about this. How does your unit work?"

"Well, the industry figures ten to fifteen percent of insurance claims are fraudulent. Actually, I think it's much higher, myself. But to cut down on fraud, save some of that money, they hire people like us. We go out and investigate suspicious claims."

"Are people paying money to themselves inside the insurance companies?"

"We don't get into that. The companies have internal auditors. What we do, we look into fraudulent claims people make under their insurance policies. People setting fire to their own property to get the insurance money, or claiming something was stolen that they never had. Or staging accidents and fake injuries. That kind of thing."

The light, watery beer was going down well with the olives. When the food arrived, they were ready for another round. "Ten more please, Fred," Don told him, holding up the fingers of both hands. He could see that he and Jim were ahead of the others, and calculated that each would need an extra glass to avoid running dry prematurely.

"Ten?" The bartender hesitated, seeing four men at the table. He was used to orders that divided evenly.

"Ten," Don confirmed with a nod, adding spontaneously, "If if that's not too high for you to count."

They all laughed, and Greg said, "Fred's okay—you can kid around with Fred. He's been here since Adam was knee-high." They sucked at the small glasses.

"This used to be our hangout when we were on the force," Don said. "We had a code name for it—the Ammo Shop."

Stefan was bemused.

"You may have noticed, this is called the Springfield Tavern," Don explained. "Springfield rifles, guns, ammo. Just a code name—so the sergeant would think we were on police business." He gave a musical laugh.

"One thing I like about fraud investigation," Greg said as they tackled the hot, spicy sandwiches, "you can get the individuals, as opposed to companies. The guy who makes the claim and stands to lose if he doesn't get away with it."

"That's right," said Don. "As detectives, we'd see so many cases where people have been shafted, but even when you nail the perpetrators, you're only nailing a company. The individuals behind it get off scot-free."

"Do you decide who to investigate?" Stefan asked.

"More or less. Anything suspicious, as well as all claims over fifty thousand, get passed to us. Then we decide what smells." He laughed again.

"You have to have a nose for it," Jim smiled.

"Do you interrogate the suspects?" Stefan asked.

Don smiled. "We try to avoid police terminology. But we have the techniques, and we have the contacts. It's teamwork. Between the police and fire departments, engineers and experts of one sort or another, the Insurance Crime Prevention Bureau, the adjuster, and ourselves, you have a real cast of characters on some of these fire losses."

"Just what the president ordered."

Don laughed, then looked at his watch. "Oh-oh," he said, "we'll have to cut this short. Drink up, Stefan."

Chamberlain was waiting in his office. Asking Stefan to close the door, he said, "Before I introduce you to the people you'll be working with, I just wanted to say again, I'd like you to report to me on anything important, including the engineering and professional liability files." He looked at Stefan, to make sure he had understood.

"By the way," he continued, "there are over five thousand files, but you won't be expected to dot the i's and cross the t's. I'm trying to save staffing costs by not having a unit of half-a-dozen people look after these files. You'll have an outside lawyer to help you as far as strategy is concerned, but there will be enough work without all those computer entries." He stood up. "Let's go up to the fifth floor, and the person you're going to meet first is Gavin Grince, the Claims Manager of the Select Risks Claims Department."

Grince was a man of about fifty, stooped, of medium build. Framed by pretty curls, his broad face had a pitted and frozen appearance, accentuated by narrowed eyes. As he came forward to shake hands, Stefan noticed that he walked on the front of his feet with a padding gait, as if trying to avoid falling forward.

"I'll leave you together," Chamberlain said after introducing them. "I have a meeting with the Choice Brokers at two."

Grince nodded eagerly. "I'm sure they'll be as easy to deal with as always," he said with a falsetto giggle.

As Chamberlain left the room, closing the door behind him, Grince turned to Stefan. "Have a seat," he said, now in a grave, formal tone, motioning towards a cream-coloured circular table in the middle of the office. Stefan noticed that there was no desk, only a counter in the same material along two of the walls. On the other side was a cabinet, in a dark green plastic material, about the size of a wardrobe.

"You'll have attended the presentation by the president," Grince continued when they were seated. He spoke in an accent that was unfamiliar to Stefan, and his speech seemed distorted, although Grince was speaking quite slowly, savouring his words. "The three principles of the company's success, as you will have heard, are service, expertise and culture, and our mission is to maximize our attainment of these principles. We are team players, and that means that we operate as an interactive group. At the same time, everybody is expected to be proactive and pragmatic. But as the leader of this unit, anything that happens here must go through me. Yep." As he spoke, Grince was constantly wiping specks of dust from the table, rubbing his hands, then flicking specks from his trousers. Stefan glimpsed his knee jigging across the table.

"This must be quite a new approach," Stefan said.

"This must be a new approach? Well, we won't go into that now." Grince's eyes narrowed even further to produce a far-seeing expression. "Yep."

Stefan listened as Grince outlined the duties of a "claims handler", which were to read, or "review", reports of new claims, decide whether the insurance policy covered the claims, and if it did, work with adjusters and others to agree the amount of damage or loss with the interested parties.

"Naturally, we don't expect you to digest all the policy wordings in one day," Grince said. "Even I can't claim to be familiar with everything. Which is why we have specialists. You'll find that we have specialists in various fields here, and there are outside experts that we use, according to the guidelines."

As Grince spoke glowingly about guidelines and corporate structure, Stefan's eyes and mouth began to feel dry, and he became aware of the stale air pervading the office. Grince himself also exuded the pungent odour of unhealthy skin.

Eventually, Grince finished his discourse and led Stefan out of his office. "I'd like you to meet the leader of our in-house claims legal department," he said. "This is a unit we've had for a few years now, to handle minor litigation and to give opinions on various questions which come up, but now they're expanding their influence." He dropped his voice meaningfully.

He padded busily towards another enclosed office, inside which they found a woman sitting behind a counter similar to Grince's. "I'd like you to meet Marlene Clewer," Grince told Stefan.

Stefan saw a plump woman in her late thirties, in a tailored suit and cravat, carefully coiffed, with a guarded smile which revealed a prominent jaw structure. As they shook hands, he caught a slightly sour powdery scent.

"Marlene is expanding her unit's horizons—and her unit," Grince said with his high-pitched giggle. Clewer thought for a moment, then smiled knowingly and said, "After a fashion."

"How many people do you have?" Stefan asked her.

"Six. We're hiring two more," she answered. She pitched her voice as low as possible, but rather than producing a commanding tone from her lower register like some women, Clewer emitted a thin bleating sound which Stefan found difficult to catch.

Stefan was introduced to some of the lawyers, all young people who had qualified in the last two or three years, then spent the next hour moving from cubicle to cubicle to meet fellow workers. Each cubicle had walls consisting of greyish cloth-covered panels which could be assembled or dismantled in minutes, the height, and the interior space, determined by the salary grade and title of the worker as set out in the corporate regulations, Grince told him. All the cubicles contained the type of counter Stefan had seen in Grince's office, with a computer terminal in front of the occupant. Many of the workers had family photographs and ornaments on a shelf near their terminal, and all had a company mug, which they could fill at a coin-operated coffee machine nearby. Behind piles of paper stacked in folders or strewn over their counter, each worker had a framed copy of the Three Principles, and the slogan, "We appreciate You", prominently displayed on a plastic stand.

A young woman came to explain to him how to use his computer, and Grince gave him a bound copy of the departmental guidelines. "I've arranged for you to spend time with Malcolm, at the next cubicle," Grince said. "He's not here today, but in the morning, he can get you started and answer any questions you may have. Okay?"

Shortly after five, as he was leaving for the day, Stefan found one of the lawyers waiting for the elevator. They recognized each other, and the lawyer, Frank Cameron, suggested a drink.

Stefan accepted. "Then I have to contact a rental agency about an apartment."

"I may be able to give you some advice about that," Frank said as they got into the elevator. They left the building by a side door, and a few minutes later were in a bar in a nearby hotel.

"Actually, I'm getting married in a few weeks," Frank continued when they had ordered. "I'm looking for somebody to sublet my apartment. We're moving into a townhouse."

"How long has the lease to run?"

"Five months. But it can be renewed after that."

"Where is the apartment?"

"You can walk it in about fifteen or twenty minutes, or take the streetcar. You can let me know." He sipped his drink. "Anyway, tell me how you found your first day at the I. P."

Stefan tried to sum up his first impressions of company life, but found he had little to say. "I guess the jury's still out," Frank said with a laugh.

"Can I ask you how you get along with Miss Clewer?" Stefan asked.

Frank smiled. "You're supposed to say 'Miz'," he said. "Well, you find you can live with most situations. As a lawyer, I'd say she's mainly smoke and mirrors. As a person, she has a reputation for being two-faced, and also she doesn't like to be corrected. Otherwise, she's fine." He laughed again.

"Don't you want to be a professional lawyer?" Stefan asked him.

"You mean in a law firm? I used to be. Right now, though, I prefer to have a life. The hours you have to put in at a law firm, to meet your quota of billable hours—it's totally unreasonable. But if you want to make it as a 'professional' lawyer, as you put it—or a 'real' lawyer, as some would say—that's part of the deal. At least here, I have the evenings and weekends."

Stefan returned to his hotel, had a snack at a coffee shop in the lobby, and went up to his room. He stood at the window for a few minutes, looking down at the lake, watching a small plane coming in to land at the island airport. Then he remembered the slip of paper the young woman had given him on the plane.

It was still in his wallet. He took it out, checked the dialling instructions on the phone and made the call.

A man's voice answered. "Ministry of Defence."

"Annette Peters, please."

"Leave your name and number, please."

He did so, then asked which base this was.

The reply was a curt, "I'll give her the message". Then the connection was cut off.

*　　　　*　　　　*

On the fifth floor of the Platinum building, Grince had just finished making notations in a new folder on his counter, labelled "Kristiansson". On a printed form, entitled "Performance Evaluation", he had pencilled in small, neat capitals, "Lacks vision and commitment. Team player characteristics not evident. Language fluency may be a problem".

It's as well to be a step ahead, Grince thought to himself as he locked the folder in his cupboard, reached for this coat and left for the day.

35

Selya looked out of the cage as it paused unexpectedly at the fifteen-hundred level. In the second or two before it regained momentum, she saw men in the tunnel, their red helmets reflecting the overhead lights. Behind them, on the tracks, was a long-hole-boring machine.

At the surface, she went straight to Martin's office. After he got off the phone, she spoke to him as calmly as she could. "Martin, what's a Kempi doing at fifteen hundred? For that matter, what are men doing there?"

Martin looked at her placidly, then held up a sheaf of printouts. "New production schedule," he said, "courtesy of Mr. Turr."

Selya thought hard. "But the level is mined out."

"There's a pocket of high-grade which was never mined."

"But it's inside the pillar. We can't mine within two hundred feet of the shaft."

"Mr. Turr has the go-ahead from the Mining Engineer's office." Seeing that she was unconvinced, Martin continued, "Look, you know we've had a good run so far, but we're now down to about forty per cent at four thousand. There may not be enough to keep us going more than a few months. We might find another vein lower down, but it's going to be more and more expensive to get out. This way we can increase our profitability and keep the bottom line healthy. Remember, close to a thousand jobs are on the line."

"Martin, I know all that. But I also know you could cause a rock-burst..."

"Don't worry. I'll make sure there's nobody underground when we blast. As you know, since Monde's accident we've used remote charges."

Selya allowed herself to be placated. But that night, she woke up with a start—and a horrible sense of foreboding.

<h1 style="text-align:center">36</h1>

As Wim came out of the terminal at Toronto's Pearson International Airport, he saw a hotel shuttle bus picking up passengers at the curb. On impulse, he joined the short line-up and climbed in. The driver closed the door, thrust the gear lever forward and pulled away. Five minutes later, he was at a hotel on the Airport Strip.

After unpacking and showering, he took the elevator to the lobby, where he had seen a car rental desk. Expecting questions and delays, he was impressed by the speed of the service. Within minutes, the representative had discussed options and prices, checked his credit card and international licence, completed the paperwork and handed him the keys to his car.

He looked the car over, then returned to the lobby and bought a map of the city. Back in his room, he looked up the Cardinal Copper Wire Company in the telephone directory. Judging by the map, it would be a half-hour's drive.

It was early in the evening, but Wim's internal clock was still set to Zambian time, six hours ahead. He threw himself on to the bed and slept.

He awoke before dawn, and went out on to the balcony. The city was still alive, a galaxy of tiny lights in the distance, but the area close by was deserted. For a few minutes, he watched traffic lights performing endlessly to an empty street.

The air was cool and fresh. It was time for a drive.

He found Cardinal's premises near the waterfront, past scrap-yards, a power station and industrial plants, at the end of a dusty, potholed road about two miles long. In his headlights, tram tracks running along the centre curved into a yard on his right, the road dead-ending at a high wooden fence. He made a u-turn and parked on the other side of the road beside a lot littered with empty fuel tanks.

The air reeked of chemicals, but he could also smell the ripe odour of the waterfront. The steady hum of electrical pylons was punctuated by shrieks of seagulls, and in the grey light, through a gap between factory buildings, he saw the silhouette of a merchant ship at berth.

He walked across the road, into Cardinal's yard. Except for a small light above a door at the corner of a grimy brick building on his left, the yard was in darkness. The door was at the top of a steel staircase.

He climbed the stairs, knocked, and immediately heard dogs barking at the rear of the building. A second later, two pit-bull terriers were snarling savagely at the foot of the staircase.

He tried the doorknob and found the door locked. It was a steel door, windowless. He put his shoulder to it, then again, but there was no movement.

One of the dogs was half-way up the stairs, menacing, its tail high. It was time to act.

He took his jacket off and rolled up his right sleeve. Then he braced himself against the top rung of the staircase, and with the jacket in his right hand, faced the animal. "Come on, boy," he said quietly.

The pit-bull was now only a leap away, its slavering jaws wide open, a ferocious snarl rising from its throat. He fixed his eyes on the dog, and at the instant it leaped forward, he flung his jacket over its head with his right hand, reaching for its collar with his left. Then, in an instant, he swept the jacket off the animal's head, thrust his right hand into its throat and grasped its tongue.

Still braced against the railing, he straightened up, pulling the dog off its front legs. At the same time, he tightened his grip on the collar, his right hand forcing the animal's tongue back into its throat. Squeezing with all his strength, he held the dog in an iron grip as it slowly choked, twisting and shuddering until it became limp. Then he let it fall down the steps.

The other dog, which had stopped barking and begun to whimper, turned and ran behind the building, its tail between its legs. Wim dusted off his hands and picked up his jacket from the steps. His right hand and forearm were scratched and bleeding, but no worse than a mineworker accepted as daily wear and tear. He threw the jacket over his shoulder, walked down the steps, grasped the dead pit-bull by the collar and dragged it to the rear of the building.

A larger building loomed at the rear, a concrete-block and corrugated-iron structure with loading bays at the side, their overhead doors closed. Wim noted two refuse containers against a wire-mesh fence, but no vehicles or trailers in the yard.

He walked around the building, climbing steps to try doors next to the loading bays. Each door was locked until he reached the last bay. He turned the knob and pulled, expecting a familiar thud from the lock, but to his surprise the door opened.

The bay was empty. He walked across to the corner, down a short flight of concrete steps, and found himself at the rear of the factory.

As his eyes adjusted to the light and he began to scan the shop floor, he heard voices. Men were coming into the building at the front.

Carefully, he backed up the steps, crossed the loading bay and left the building without being seen. A few steps took him to the refuse containers. He hoisted himself on to the edge of one of the containers, vaulted over the fence into a vacant lot, and made his way back to the road.

He drove towards the city, stopped at a gas station to clean up, then parked on a lot opposite offering a special all-day flat rate for "early bird" customers. Jokingly, he asked the attendant whether it was early enough. It was twenty minutes past six.

A pall of smog cut off his view of the CN Tower and the top of the downtown skyscrapers, about two miles straight ahead. He walked half a mile, then stopped at a restaurant for breakfast.

He had seen equipment and product in the factory, but no night shift, no vehicles in the yard, and security had been minimal. Cardinal appeared to be running a modest business at best. Unless it had other locations or assets, Wim doubted the company could be worth forty-five million Canadian dollars.

The waitress refilled his cup. He watched a streetcar sail slowly past the window, and reviewed his agenda.

Wim knew from experience that casual conversation between business associates often yielded more information than balance sheets and annual reports. While he promoted Zambian copper as a representative of ZEDA, he would have a natural opening to discuss the local players, to round out what he had seen of Cardinal's operation so far.

The local Board of Trade and the Copper Manufacturers' Association would have lists of companies and contacts. He would make a short list of prospects, then telephone to make appointments.

He left the restaurant and followed the crowds towards the heart of the city. Eventually he found a telephone stand, checked the Yellow Pages, and asked a passer-by for directions.

He was standing at a red light waiting to cross an intersection, close to the cluster of office towers which was to be his first stop, when a stream of pedestrians passed behind him from his right. Suddenly, in the hubbub of conversation, he thought he heard a familiar voice. He turned quickly to his left, and to his amazement recognized the tall, bespectacled figure of Stefan Kristiansson, deep in conversation with another man, hurrying on with the crowd.

Wim shouldered his way out of the throng, and followed.

37

Stefan had been at his desk ten minutes when his telephone
rang. "For God's sake, what's a man like you doing in a place
like that?" a familiar voice bantered.

"Wim!" Stefan laughed. "Where are you? How did you find
me here?"

"I saw you in the street, mate. I saw you go into that building."

"How did you know I was working here?"

"I didn't. But it was eight in the morning, and you had a
haunted look."

Grince, padding past the cubicles, heard Stefan laugh and cast a
pained glance in his direction, to convey that the levity, contrast-
ing with his own weighty thoughts, had been noted.

Lowering his voice, Stefan arranged to meet Wim at noon.
Then, despite his excitement, he became immersed in his work,
reading reports, taking calls, returning messages, making entries
and writing correspondence on his terminal, speaking with colleagues and members of other departments, hurrying back and
forth to the fax and copy machines.

Wim was waiting across the street at noon. "What in God's
name..." he began when they were seated in the restaurant.

Stefan explained. "At least I'm seeing the world," he smiled weakly.

Wim told him how he came to be in Toronto. "I get the impression there's more to this than meets the eye," he added.

"Why do you think that?"

"Well, I can see the government wanting to keep the lid on this. It would be embarrassing if it got out that somebody had stolen fifty billion kwachas under their nose. So I can see the DNS handling it. But Paxton seems to be working outside the DNS."

"He may have been told to handle it personally."

Wim thought for a moment. "You may be right," he said.

They talked about the mine, and Stefan mentioned his conversation with Thacker.

Wim looked skeptical. "I was never impressed by Thacker. If we could get an independent survey done...but it's not likely to happen. Paxton can do nothing."

He remembered that Paxton had spoken of Selya, and asked Stefan whether he had been in touch with her.

"Only by E-mail, and in an indirect way," Stefan answered. "Since I've been in Toronto, I've tried to reach her by phone two or three times, but I haven't heard back."

"Unfortunately, I can't risk trying to communicate with anybody over there myself, at least until Paxton has the charges against me dropped. Reading between the lines, that will depend on the success of this mission." Wim described what he had seen at Cardinal's premises, and outlined how he planned to continue his investigation.

It was time for Stefan to get back to work. Wim wrote down his hotel telephone number on a napkin and gave it to him. "Try to reach me tonight," he said.

A few minutes after Stefan got back to his desk, Grince appeared at the entrance to his cubicle. "Do you have a minute?" he asked brusquely.

Stefan nodded, expecting Grince to go on. But Grince was padding towards his office, and Stefan realized he was expected to follow.

"Close the door." Grince chose a tone designed to convey pre-occupation with important affairs. "There are one or two things we need to discuss," he added briskly, his eyes narrowed towards some distant horizon, busily rolling a chair up to his table.

"As you know, we have a flexible-hours procedure in this company. It's something I have reservations about personally, but so far I haven't had much success at rescinding it." His voice rose at the end of the sentence, with a slight gasp to convey frustration and amusement at the failure of others to see the light. He recalled his early days in a government office in Glasgow, where employees had signed a ledger as they arrived in the morning. At nine precisely, the manager would draw a line across the page, exposing those who came in later to a "carpeting" in his office. Scrupulously punctual himself, Grince had eventually been assigned to stand watch over the signers-in and to draw the line at the appointed time, the hint of a smirk behind his pious expression as he scrutinized latecomers' faces for signs of fear. It had been one of the defining moments in his career.

"As you also know, this procedure operates on an honour system, in a teamwork context." Grince relished the words against his palate. "Consistent with our corporate culture, a quota of fifty percent of the unit is required by the guidelines to be at their desks at all times." He wiped some flecks of dust from the table, swept them off his trousers with the back of his hand, then rubbed his hands together with an abrasive flourish.

"When you went to lunch today, for an hour and ten minutes, did you verify that the required quota would be in place in the office?"

Stefan was taken aback. He had understood that Grince had been told by other members of the department that his "quota" concept was unworkable. Staff were frequently out of the office on business, often at short notice. No quota could be guaranteed.

Rather than point this out, Stefan made a self-deprecating comment to the effect that he doubted he could deal with his colleagues' work in any event.

"You wouldn't be able to deal with their work?" Grince echoed his words, his voice rising to a note of derision. "But that's not the point. Even if the particular issues can not be resolved at the time," he said slowly and condescendingly, "the guidelines require a quota in the office at all times, to take calls as required. And as I understand it, you neglected to ensure that the unit was covered before taking an extended lunch break." He stared at Stefan, as if challenging him to respond.

Stefan sensed that Grince was determined to pursue the point *ad nauseam*, and said no more.

"One other matter that I apparently need to bring to your attention:" Grince continued, "obviously we need to document the files properly, so that if anything happened to you, other people would be able to determine the status. Unfortunately, when I look at the computer notes on your engineering and professional files, in the vast majority of cases there are very few entries if any."

"There are over five thousand of those files." Again Stefan was taken by surprise. "There is no time to enter computer notes in so many cases. I also have three hundred other files. This is surely common sense."

Grince stiffened, then affected a tolerant expression. "I recognize that there are quite a number of files." He gave a slight smile and shake of the head, to indicate how difficult it was at times to get through to people. "But there are standards to maintain. It's not a matter of common sense. It's a matter of proper claims handling procedure. Yep."

Grince's eyes were fixed on Stefan, waiting for another chance to continue the debate. The tight smirk flashed an unmistakable message: the longer you resist, the more enjoyable this is going to be.

Stefan looked away. He realized that if he persisted, Grince would be able to characterize him as argumentative, and he hesitated to invoke Chamberlain. "I'll do whatever I can," he said, hiding his distaste.

A few minutes later, Grince closed the meeting with a loud, dismissive "Thank you," drowning Stefan's polite leave-taking with an equally loud "Good." Stefan left Grince's office and gulped the marginally less stale air outside.

*　　　*　　　*

Upstairs in the boardroom, an advertising agency was about to show the new television commercial to a group of vice-presidents. "The ad was designed to combine a sense of your company's leadership in today's high-tech world, "an agency representative intoned, "with your long history of service to the community."

The lights dimmed, and the advertisement appeared on the screen. Against a dramatic spectacle of burning buildings, wreckages of vehicles in a highway disaster, and houses demolished in a tornado, the Imperial Platinum logo loomed into the centre of the screen, and a simpering voice was heard in the background. "For a hundred and fifty years," it quavered, "we have been standing by, ready to lend a helping hand in times of need. A company you can trust, because we have always been there for you. A company which has always believed in fair play, because that's the way you want us to be. A company with vision, in the forefront of our high-tech world, but proud of our history. Moving forward for you for a hundred and fifty years".

The lights came back on, and the executives were seen nodding approval, basking in the glamour of the production. "Could positively impact our image," one woman said in a loud, coarse voice. "And the out-turn," a man replied. "Right, it could help us grow our book of business," enthused another. "Liked the laid-back voice," the woman added. "Non-threatening. No pressure."

"The way all men should be, eh Barbara?" one of the men bantered.

"We used the same voice in an automobile commercial," the agency representative said. "The one where we focus on the sensible, no-frills approach."

There were murmurs of recognition. "Appeals to the thinking consumer," one of the executives said approvingly.

As they filed out of the door, one of the men said to another, "Wasn't quite sure about the history-of-moving-forward-for-you bit. Back in the nineteenth century, I would have thought the idea would be to take in as much money as possible, and pay out as little as possible."

"I thought that was still the idea," the other quipped.

They both laughed. "Well, that profit-sharing bonus certainly helps," the first said.

The woman Barbara took the elevator to the parking garage. Later that day she was to fly to the west coast, to visit a branch. She would drive home in her Cadillac, then take a limousine to the airport.

On the way down, employees who got into the elevator quickly converted their wide-eyed awe at the sight of an executive into eager, dutiful and contented expressions. Her eyes ever-watchful, Barbara absorbed the homage. But one man got into the elevator who did not seem to observe this ritual of subservience, a man whose pupils did not dilate when he saw her, who did not look away quickly, but who appraised her calmly and objectively as though he were passing a stranger on the street. He must be the man Fraser Chamberlain brought in, she thought. Christopherson, or some name like that. She made a mental note of his face.

*   *   *

During the afternoon, a young man came to replace Stefan's computer with a new model. "Something to do with the latest software," Malcolm called out from the next cubicle. "I got mine yesterday. You'll need two passwords now. A girl will be coming over to go through the drill."

While he was waiting, Stefan noticed a flashing light on his telephone, and realised he had messages. He entered his codes and listened.

The first two were from insurance people. A reinsurance company representative was calling to find out how a large claim was progressing, and someone in the claims department of an insurance brokerage was calling to hurry a client's claim along. Stefan noted the names and telephone numbers.

The third message was a pleasant surprise. "This is Corporal Peters," the voice said. "I was away for a while—just got your message. Give me a call when you have a chance."

38

Martin sent his weekly report to Turr by internal E-mail, then leaned back, swivelled around and stretched contentedly. The high-grade ore was more than making up for the marginal results in the main development section. He could see three months' work at fifteen-hundred, after which the stopes would be safely sealed, and they would move to another high-grade pocket at nineteen-hundred feet.

The last rings had been blasted three hours ago, shortly after three in the afternoon, and while there had been some predictable tremors, the shaft had not been damaged. Crews would work through the evening and night to get the ore to the crushers and clean up for the next shift. He backed out of his computer and began to tidy his desk.

It began as a rumble of distant thunder, swelling in seconds to an unearthly roar. Desks and windows began to rattle, quietly at first, then more violently until shock-waves buffetted his ear drums. He grasped the edge of his desk, his mind trying to block out the unspeakable reality which was tearing him apart internally. Dimly, he heard shouting, screaming, an explosion, then another. His door blew open, and he caught a blast of stale, dusty air smelling of rotten eggs. Then the power failed.

In slow motion, he forced himself to his feet, struggling against an immense weight that seemed to be crushing his chest. Drenched in cold sweat, he tried to reach for the telephone, but something seemed to be holding his arm down. He felt his legs go numb, and heard a singing in his ears as darkness closed in around him.

For ten minutes, rancid mud and slime gushed into the mine through a funnel crater that had burst open below the tailings pond. Half a million cubic yards of saturated sand, silt, earth and decayed vegetation poured through the maze of horizontal and vertical arteries surrounding the main shaft. It roared along the tunnels and down the winzes, unpredictable and unstoppable, hurling and smashing heavy equipment like flotsam, rolling in a giant wave over men caught in its path before they could move or cry out.

It stopped as suddenly as it had begun, and the darkness became eerily quiet, the unhurried dripping of water in the tunnels and the eternal creaking of the mine the only audible sounds. Then, from the shocked silence, voices—the voices growing louder and more intense as the men realized that power had been cut not only to the hoists but also to the pumps. Desperate to escape the rising water below, men began to climb up the main and auxiliary shafts.

At the surface, there was controlled panic. The rescue team on call prepared to climb down the main shaft to make a preliminary survey, and electrical engineers began work feverishly to restore power. One of the two ambulances was already on the road to Lusaka with Martin, leaving Morag alone in the clinic, since the other three first-aiders were somewhere below surface. Eucalyptus oil, the traditional signal to evacuate, was poured down all the vertical ventilation shafts, to clear both affected and unaffected areas of the mine, so that the number of missing workers could be established.

Two hours later, the rescue team reported that mud and water had flooded five levels at and below fifteen-hundred feet. Mud and debris, including ore fragments, boulders, soil, silt and mine equipment, had flowed horizontally three thousand feet along the tunnels. In those areas, the team felt that no workers could have survived.

While the first rescue team was underground, the mine captain, Martin's deputy, called three mines within a radius of thirty miles to ask for help. Each responded within hours with two rescue teams, and during the first night over a hundred men were brought to surface. But there was still no estimate of the death toll.

*   *   *

Four thousand feet below, buried in sludge above her waist, her left foot pinned by an overturned cart, Selya strained to free herself, her hands against the wall behind her. She had been swept along the tunnel into a refuge bay on the outside of a curve, and the cart had slammed against the wall, spun around into the bay and blocked her in.

Her foot was numb, but she could feel the rim of the cart biting into her ankle at the top of her work boot. She tried to move her right foot towards the cart, to push it away or lever it off her left foot, but when she did so she lost her balance and slid down the wall.

She fought to keep her head above the sludge, gasping with shock. She managed to get her right foot underneath her again and work her way back against the wall. Her head throbbing from the pain in her ankle, she tried to collect her thoughts.

She thought she heard voices, and cried out, but there was no reply. She cried out again, and again, until her throat was dry and raw. When she stopped, the only sound she heard was the dripping of water, unrelenting and impervious.

But the water seemed to be dripping more loudly now, echoing with a new resonance. Terrified, she realized that the pumps had failed, and that the water in the shafts had reached her level. In less than an hour, it would be over her head.

She knew she had to try again. She felt her arms could not hold on to the wall much longer, and she had strength for only one more attempt. This time she would have to heave herself forward, go down on her right knee and get both hands under the rim of the cart.

She spent a few minutes rehearsing the movement in her mind, trying to gather strength mentally and physically. Then she took a deep breath, pushed herself away from the wall, and sank into the sludge.

She closed her eyes and felt her head go under. Her right knee reached the ground, and her left hand found the trapped boot. Now she had both hands under the cart. Desperately, she heaved, but the cart did not move. Again she tried, and again. Defeated, she pushed herself upright, surfaced, and threw herself forward on to the upturned underbelly of the cart, gasping for air. Then she passed out.

<h1 style="text-align:center">39</h1>

As time passed, people at Imperial Platinum came to see Stefan as a useful source of advice, frequently calling him to discuss policy wordings and claims. While claims people usually had to decide whether or not a wording covered an actual claim, for underwriters the question tended to be whether a wording might cover potential claims they had not envisaged or did not want to cover, and if so, how the wording could be satisfactorily amended.

Stefan had seen that insurance wordings could be dissected as meticulously by insurers and insureds as ancient manuscripts and inscriptions were by scholars. Unlike academic disputes, however, differences of opinion over insurance verbiage tended to be resolved either by the authority of a judge or arbitrator, or by compromise. In helping his colleagues, Stefan often searched the indices and databases for judicial decisions on the point at issue, and he did this despite having come to realize that the wordings were apt to become irrelevant if an influential broker lobbied to have a claim paid, or if it became apparent that the claim could be settled for less than the amount the insurer would otherwise have to pay in legal fees to defend a lawsuit.

Don Gibson, who chaired a committee of insurers concerned about the cost of fraud, asked Stefan to speak at a gathering of investigators, lawyers and insurance workers about the engineer's role in detecting deliberately-set fires and staged accidents, and in reconstructing accident and fire scenes. One of Don's committee members asked Stefan to write a series of articles on the subject for a trade publication, a task which kept him occupied into the early hours for several months. He was rewarded for his efforts with a note from the president: "Thanks, Stefan, for getting involved. This is teamwork at its best."

"Congratulations," Chamberlain told him. "Your hard work is paying off." Despite the danger his presence had created, Chamberlain admired Stefan as someone apparently uninterested in office politics, someone who simply enjoyed dealing with work and problems, who never missed a day at the office, and who seemed to run continuously like a machine. Stefan had also blended in well, and in any event the danger would soon be over.

Shortly afterwards, Grince handed out a schedule of appointments headed "Performance Evaluation".

"Time for your audience," Malcolm joked as Stefan headed towards Grince's office at the appointed hour.

"Close the door." Grince continued to study a file in front of him. Eventually, he looked up and said, "I assume you know what this is about. We're here to discuss your performance." He studied Stefan for signs of intimidation.

Stefan looked at him, waiting.

"Obviously, we have a few things to discuss," Grince continued. "But first, we have to evaluate your Personal Development. I'd like you to give me some examples of how you have developed your skills and used them to the benefit of the company since you have been with us." He seemed to enjoy enunciating the word "skills", relishing its officious ring as it exercised his lips and tongue.

Stefan looked past Grince at another office-building across the street, glass and steel reflecting brilliant sunlight. He wondered what Grince understood by the term, "personal development". He mentioned several contentious claims which his technical knowledge had helped to settle, and he cited the work he had done, on his own time, for the committee of insurers. "I also spend a lot of my time helping people who have questions of one sort or another," he added, "and I've received letters of thanks from people, for dealing with their claims promptly and fairly." Although he prided himself on his ability to cope with pressure, he saw no need to mention his phenomenal volume of claims, since statistics of each worker's caseload were regularly circulated throughout the department.

Grince assumed a thoughtful pose. He began to make a note, then stopped and said, "Now I'd like to discuss the professional liability files. We have to maintain these files according to the procedures laid out in the guidelines. Your performance in this area gives me cause for concern." He began to cite the clerical procedures which, as Chamberlain had pointed out, were obviously out of the question while the company saved staffing costs by assigning a single individual to a portfolio of several thousand files.

Stefan gazed at Grince in disbelief. Both he and Chamberlain had pointed out the facts to Grince on more than one occasion. He began to wonder whether Grince was playing some kind of game, or whether some psychological dysfunction made him regress to his original position however often he was corrected.

Stefan hesitated to invoke Chamberlain's authority, but at the same time felt that to argue the matter yet again would both dignify Grince and put himself on the defensive. He simply made a note and said nothing. It crossed his mind that Chamberlain could settle the matter by confirming his instructions in writing. But people resent being asked to confirm something they have said in writing, Stefan thought, and he was inclined to avoid offending Chamberlain.

"Another matter which we need to discuss," Grince continued, "is the Poxidyl Corporation file. You have apparently agreed to attend the trial, assuming of course that the claim is not settled in the interim."

"Certain days. Don and I would be alternating. Legal counsel think we should be there in person, so that the judge sees that we are not remote, faceless people. The issues are quite complicated."

"For someone who claims to be so burdened with work, it's somewhat surprising that you're perfectly happy to spend six weeks in a courtroom." With his tight-lipped smirk, Grince delivered the line he'd been rehearsing for a week.

Stefan resisted the temptation to react to the sarcasm, or to argue defensively that his time in court would be in the company's interests, in a five-million-dollar lawsuit that might hinge on a judge's perception. "I think we expect to spend ten days in court, over a three-week period," he said, his voice flat. "Ten days between Don and myself."

"The length of the trial is neither here nor there," Grince said. "The fact is that you are quite happy to be out of the office for a protracted period."

"I expect to be here on alternate days."

"But you are expecting the rest of the team to cover for you on the other days."

Stefan was about to say that he would be calling in, as always, to deal with messages and problems, when he remembered his decision not to be drawn into a defensive position. Trying to keep his face expressionless, he waited until Grince had finished and he was able to leave.

As he was passing the filing racks in the centre of the office, he met one of his colleagues, Anne Mowbray, who gave him a searching look. "You look tired, Stefan," she said.

He looked at her, tried to smile, but could say nothing.

"Come on, let it out," she said.

After he had said a few words, she held up her hand. "Stefan," she said, "Gavin has made a career out of selecting people to demoralize. Just think how lucky you are not to be a long-term employee with a mortgage and a pension on the line." She laughed wryly, then continued, "Everybody knows your workload is double what you should be carrying, and we all wonder how on earth you do it. And attending the trial—it's not as if it's a vacation. This is a duty, something which you've been asked to do for the good of the company." She shook her head incredulously.

"Surely this man does not fit the 'culture' we are hearing about," Stefan said.

"No, you're absolutely right." She dropped her voice. "And I think other people can see that. But for some reason Clive arranged to move him into this department. The strange thing is that Clive told us quite recently that he disliked Gavin and could never work with him."

"He said that?"

"They had crossed paths a few times over the years, when Clive was in a less senior position. He knew Gavin, and he knew he would never change. 'Leopards don't change their spots', was the phrase he used. But not to fear, he said, Gavin would never come into this department."

"So what happened to make him renege on his promise?"

"I really don't know," she said slowly, emphasizing each word.

Stefan closed his eyes and shook his head. He returned to his desk and worked compulsively for the rest of the afternoon, trying to ignore a sharp pain in the back of his head, behind his right ear.

*   *   *

Upstairs on the executive floor, Barbara Fleam and Marlene Clewer were sitting on a sofa in Fleam's office, a ten-by-twenty foot enclave walled off more permanently than the plebeian cubicles outside, and further distinguished by deep carpeting, mahogany furniture, shaded lamps and oil paintings. The office occupied a corner of the building with a view of the harbour and its trendy restaurants and boutiques. It was a setting which encouraged feelings of lofty superiority.

"Of course, Clive Chamberlain only has a couple of years to go," Fleam was saying. "So when Jenner moves to New York, you know who could become the first woman president here."

"Not before time," said Clewer.

Stone-faced and slightly flushed at the prospect of power, Fleam squirmed impatiently. Her mouth, chronically set in a cruel slant except when she was in the president's company, became mobile again as she continued. "I've spoken to Clive," she declaimed, "and he agrees that you should continue to expand your sphere of influence. Of course, Clive doesn't know this, but I'd like you to take over his job when he retires in a year or two, assuming everything goes as planned."

Clewer's eyes opened wide, and she stiffened. She began to babble words of gratitude and loyalty, but Fleam held up her hand. "I just wanted you to know," she said, "so you can get your ducks in order." She reached over and squeezed Clewer's thigh.

"Speaking of ducks," Fleam continued, pausing to let Clewer register dutiful amusement, "as you may know, I've never had much use for men in my departments. I may keep the odd token male, but that's it."

"Now I want you to look around, take stock. No need to do anything right away, you understand. Just keep me posted, so we can be making plans."

She smoothed her skirt, then lifted her hand to dismiss the topic. "Now. Back to the employee appreciation day," she said briskly. "We want you to do a presentation about your unit. The number of cases you handle, the cost of handling them in-house compared to outside lawyers, and the average time to dispose of them. Clive will let you know officially, since you're still in his baileywick, but I thought I'd let you know I've arranged it with the president."

"I'll get started on it right away," said Clewer.

"Of course we know the difficult cases go to outside counsel, so it's apples and oranges, but most people won't know that. It'll be good exposure for you."

Clewer left Fleam's office with a new sense of purpose and inner strength. She now saw herself as more than a cog, however privileged, in a bureaucratic institution. She was now part of a new order, with access to the inner circle.

Fleam congratulated herself. She saw Clewer as a lawyer trained to serve clients' interests. She would serve a president and mentor with even more unswerving devotion.

As she was leaving, Clewer had a thought. She turned and said, "Stefan Kristiansson strikes me as someone who needs to be watched."

"Yes."

"He has made quite a name for himself, in a short time."

"He's Clive's man, isn't he?"

"I think so."

"What have you got on him?"

"He works very well with all the players, gets on with people in the company, gets involved in various committees. My people think well of him. Actually, talking of teams, I understand he played hockey on his university team in Sweden. Then in southern Africa he learned to play cricket, and captained a team at one point. So it might be difficult to say he's not a team player."

At the mention of cricket, Fleam's mouth twiched in a derisive smirk. "Don't be too sure what we can say or can't say," she said.

"I *have* heard that he finds Grince obnoxious."

"Well, now, I can see a lot of possibilities there. A *lot* of possibilities. This could be your chance to get off the ground. Think about it and keep me posted."

40

During his first week in Toronto, Wim visited manufacturers of copper products, discussing prices, quantities and delivery schedules, noting requirements and promising further contact from Zambian exporters. His direct, unaffected manner and his technical and practical knowledge impressed company owners, presidents, production managers and buyers alike. Without exception, they talked openly about their competitors—their products, profitability and prospects, and the people in charge. But about Cardinal, they had no current information.

"They did tell me that for years, Cardinal used to produce wire for power station transformers," Wim told Stefan. "But how the business is doing now, and who is behind it, nobody knows for sure."

"If you give me the names of the officers of the company, I may be able to help," Stefan said. "Insurance companies are always investigating people, and some of our staff investigators have police contacts."

Wim looked at his notes. "I've got Frank James as president, and Caspar Lorel as secretary/treasurer." He began to copy out the names and addresses. "It's worth a try," he told Stefan, "but there should be no direct contact or surveillance. I'll do that myself if I have to."

Don Gibson took less than an hour to report back to Stefan the next day. "They have nothing on James," he said, "but this Lorel character has a rap-sheet going back about fifteen years, and he's done time for embezzlement and exortion."

In the archives of the *Globe and Mail* the next day, Wim checked the stock quotations and scanned the business sections for references to Cardinal. Going back five years, he found the company's shares trading on the Toronto Stock Exchange between seven and eight dollars, a range that was maintained for the next two years. The share value then dropped steeply, first below three dollars, then below two, then to sixty cents.

Wim asked to speak with an editor of the business section. He was shown into a general office and asked to take a seat. Five minutes later, a young man in shirtsleeves came out to see him. "Mike Gerrard," he said as Wim introduced himself.

"Let me save you some time," Gerrard said after Wim explained what he was looking for. "Come over to my desk. I'll see what we have on the system."

Two minutes later, they had part of the answer. Three years ago, Cardinal had lost its transformer business. "It's back to the drawing board," Frank James was quoted as saying. "We're actively considering all our options at this stage."

Gerrard scrolled down the screen. "There's nothing further on Cardinal until the news release on the take-over, a few months ago."

"Can you tell who ended up with the controlling interest?"

"Let me give you a name to call." Gerrard flipped through his address book, made a note on the back of a business card and handed it to Wim. "Remember to call me if you find anything," he said as he saw Wim to the door.

Gerrard's contact was a secretarial assistant at the Stock Exchange, who faxed Wim a series of printouts the next day. He pored over them in his hotel room.

As he studied the trades, Wim saw that James had increased his holding from seventeen to twenty-four per cent of the outstanding shares after the value had dropped to sixty cents. At the same time, Caspar Lorel, over a period of three or four months, had bought seventy-one per cent. This left only five per cent in the hands of minority shareholders.

At that point, Wim realized, the company was effectively owned by Lorel, who then had a free hand to open the door to the Zambians. Lorel would have paid off James and the minority shareholders, taken his own cut, then transferred the balance to private accounts.

Wim outlined his theory to Stefan that evening. "When James lost his main customer," he said, "he found another way to stay alive, and profit at the same time. On paper, he still had a viable operation. It was perfect for money-laundering."

"And he also kept his job as president."

"Yes, he'll be running a token operation, helping Lorel to cook the books."

"But foreign investors may have to obtain clearance from the Canadian government," Stefan suggested.

"I've checked. There's a threshold, just under two hundred mil. Over that, a review board carries out an inquiry. Otherwise, if the price seems reasonable, and the investors have good credentials, it's likely to get rubber-stamped. In this case, the offer was in the middle of a fairly recent trading range, and the business was solvent and operational—so it would look legitimate enough on paper."

"What about the investors?"

"Anybody with access to that kind of money in Zambia would command the best references in the country. In fact, they might even *be* the best references."

Wim leaned back in his chair. "Before Lorel came on the scene, there was one shareholder with over thirty per cent of the company," he thought aloud. "Maybe she can tell me something."

Mrs. Hazel Overend lived in an exclusive retirement residence in a pleasant suburban neighbourhood just north of the city. At the end of a cul-de-sac, elegant landscaping led to an entrance and lobby which might have graced a country club. Through picture-windows at the far side, Wim could see a waterfall in a leafy garden court ringed by park benches.

Accompanied by a young woman at a grand piano, about two dozen residents were singing lustily, "Let me call you sweetheart". Another woman stood at a microphone, leading the festivities. Wim took a seat at the back, joining in as the selection continued with "Bill Bailey", "Keep the home fires burning", and "Easter Parade".

When the sing-along ended and the residents began to move away, an elderly man came up to him. "You know," he cried, "the lodge pays these people to come here, and that's okay, but I wonder whether they think we're all about a hundred and ten, the songs they come up with."

Wim smiled. "I thought you managed them very well," he said.

"You're not selling life insurance, by any chance?" the man continued with a twinkle.

"No, I came to see Mrs. Overend," Wim laughed.

"Hazel? She was right here..." He hailed one of the retreating residents, who turned and smiled, happy to have a visitor.

Mrs. Overend was a well-manicured, blue-rinsed eighty-year-old with an air of old money. "My husband was president of the Commercial Bank," she told Wim almost immediately. "He provided for me very well."

She had inherited the shares along with her husband's other investments. "I never paid any attention to those things," she said with a restrained wave of the hand, "so I don't know what I can tell you. You say you're looking into the company?"

"Yes, ma'am. My assocation represents the copper industry, and we're interested when a company like Cardinal changes hands. Your husband was a major shareholder."

"He may have been, but if he ever mentioned the name, I don't recall."

"Do you remember how you came to sell the shares?"

Mrs. Overend's face brightened. "That I do remember. It was about a year ago. A young man came to see me, like yourself. He said the company president wanted to retire, I recall. He wanted to find a buyer to carry on after he retired, but he needed a large number of shares—what would you call it…"

Wim thought for a moment. "A controlling interest?"

"I think so. If he could get enough shares together, he might be able to interest someone in buying the company."

"Did he discuss the price?"

"Well, I just remember he said it wasn't public knowledge yet that Mr. …"

"Mr. James?"

"…the company president…yes, that may have been the name. He was trying to help the shareholders by keeping quiet about the fact that he was planning to retire. He thought the price would go down if people found out."

"Because he had built up the company, you mean?"

Mrs. Overend nodded. "That part I could understand. I remember my husband kept his retirement plans a secret for a long time, until the next president was ready to take over. I had to act as if nothing was in the works." She chuckled to herself at the memory.

"People have more confidence in someone they've known for a long time."

Mrs. Overend, still smiling, nodded. "Anyway, the price was...I forget the figure, but that's what the shareholders were being offered. Otherwise, if he had to retire without finding a buyer..." She left the sentence unfinished.

"Do you remember whether this man was a company representative..."

"He was a stockbroker. Oh yes, I checked who he was, and I had our accountant check the price and take care of everything. Then I signed the certificates and he gave me a certified cheque."

After hearing similar accounts from other ex-shareholders, Wim reported to Arnald by fax, and three days later, they spoke by telephone. "You've given us some useful information," Arnald said. "The stockbroker clearly misled the shareholders. He wasn't trying to get James a controlling interest, so that James could then look for a buyer. His client was Lorel, not James, and Lorel already had a buyer waiting in the wings. In effect, the stockbroker was helping Lorel to pave the way for the Zambians, who could then make a formal offer at the pre-arranged price and establish a legitimate conduit for the money."

Wim sucked in his breath. "Would you like me to track down James and Lorel?"

"We have a few things to sort out first. We've asked the Canadian government to have their foreign investment review board take another look at Cardinal, and we're trying to get the local Securities Commission to investigate the stockbroker. In the meantime, I think you should stay in Toronto, in case these people want to speak to you, but do nothing else unless you hear from me."

Arnald saw no need to add that Paxton, on the strength of Wim's reports, had launched a financial investigation of Mukuba and his associates, and had traced bank transfers between Zambia, the U.K. and Canada linking Lorel's share acquisitions with the Zambians. Nor was there any need to tell him that the ultimate purpose of the exercise, the ousting of the Mpetu regime, was now on the verge of fruition.

It was five minutes to seven. The scent of freshly-mown grass wafted through the open window from the quadrangle below. Arnald glanced down at undergraduates heading towards the stone steps beneath the clock, on their way to dinner in the Great Hall. He felt grateful to be isolated from the chaos of the world beyond, in particular the imminent upheaval in Zambia which he had helped to engineer. With a euphoric sigh, he closed his eyes and savoured the fresh, halcyon breeze.

4I

The coup was swift and relatively bloodless. Overnight, troops took over the airport, the main arteries leading into the capital, the State House and the media. The leader, Captain Polo Luonda, appeared on television at six in the morning to announce that he was now head of state, and that members of the former corrupt government had been arrested. He promised to restore civil liberties as soon as possible, but in the meantime a twenty-four-hour curfew was in effect.

Within the hour, other African states had begun to recognize the new regime in Zambia, and international recognition followed as the day wore on. Foreign correspondents inferred from the smooth transition of power, and the prompt recognition, that the coup had been planned with outside assistance.

Colonel Paxton, who with help from Wim and Arnold had put together the information Luonda needed to denounce the Mpetu regime, was hailed as a national hero. Now he would have a free hand to settle the score with Tibuluma.

But for Paxton the timing could not have been worse. The day before the coup, he had been told of the disaster at Empendwe. Over two hundred were missing, Selya among them.

Meetings with Luonda and members of the new administration kept Paxton at the State House until late evening, and it was almost midnight when he reached Empendwe. He asked for the mine manager, and was directed to the clinic, where he found the mine captain with Morag.

"So far, we have accounted for about half the personnel below surface," the captain told Paxton. "The rescue teams have made twelve investigations so far, and have brought fifty four to surface, leaving a hundred and forty three still unaccounted for. Over a hundred got out under their own steam."

"Is there any word about my daughter?"

The captain had been dreading this moment. "I'm sorry, Mr.Paxton. She was working quite far down, we think at four thousand feet. One team has been down to that level, but they could only get part way along the crosscut. It may take some time before we can get the equipment in to clear a path."

"Take me down there. I have to find her."

"Mr. Paxton, only the rescue teams are equipped to go down there. The conditions are extremely dangerous."

"I have to find her. I have to find her, man."

Paxton's voice was controlled, but so intense that the captain saw that further argument would be futile. "All right, sir," he said quickly. "I'll call up one of the teams to go with you. But you will have to change. Follow me, please."

Dressed in yellow waterproof suits equipped with oxygen packs, Paxton and five other men were winched down to four thousand level. By the light of their helmet lamps, augmented by lanterns, they climbed out of the bucket on to the stage and began to wade through mud and debris into the tunnel.

A grotesque scene confronted them. Uprooted track, littered with overturned carts and mangled pieces of machinery, poked through the mud. Conduit and cable snaked from the walls in all directions. Brackets dangled like claws from the roof, the pipes and ducts they had held ripped out of their grasp. The wreckage was covered with a thick blanket of mud and slime, and the clamminess and the stench made the men thankful for the oxygen they were carrying.

Rivulets of watery sludge were running alongside both walls toward the main shaft, and a water mark about four feet high told the men that the tunnel had flooded while the pumps were disabled. The rescuers exchanged grim glances through their plastic visors.

But Paxton, a man obsessed, was already trampling through the wreckage. The other men, heavy-hearted, followed.

They found her at the bend in the tunnel, slumped against the wall. They heaved the overturned cart upright, and Paxton knelt down to touch her ashen face.

There was no pulse. He lifted her over his shoulder, hoping to drain the water from her lungs, then laid her down and tried to breath air into her. One of the rescue team stepped forward to assist, and for ten minutes they worked desperately to revive her.

But the men knew that there was no hope. Even if her heart and lungs could have been resuscitated, her brain, deprived so long of oxygen, would have been dead.

Eventually, Paxton lifted her up and began the grim trek back along the tunnel. "She was my only family," he said, more to himself than to the others.

*   *   *

After following the ambulance to the hospital and speaking with senior staff, Paxton drove to the State House, went up to his office and closed the door. Then he sat in the darkness, his eyes closed, his hands on his desk, fighting his emotion.

To keep his mind on factual matters, he tried to recall what Selya and Wim had told him about the mine. For over an hour, he turned their comments over in his mind, returning again and again to the same questions. The Mining Engineer had been told that the mine had a history of instability, but after examining survey drawings he had allowed the mine to carry on. The drawings had seemed to support the belief that if the ground under the tailings pond collapsed, only the section of the mine which had been abandoned and sealed would be inundated. But that prediction had proved to be incorrect. Were the drawings inaccurate then, or was the Mining Engineer's interpretation of them faulty? Why also did the Mining Engineer rely on old drawings, rather than having the data verified by a new survey? And the old drawings had apparently belonged to the previous owner. Surely the present owner had ordered a survey before making an offer to purchase the mine. Why was this survey not produced?

Paxton realized he had to see the Mining Engineer's file. He unlocked a drawer in his desk and took out a set of keys, then left his office and made his way toward the other side of the building.

When he arrived two hours later, the Mining Engineer found Paxton waiting for him in his office, reading one of his files. He made no effort to hide his surprise, but his indignation evaporated when he saw the ghastly expression on Paxton's unshaven, sweaty face. "That's one of Thacker's files," he said softly, noting that the number on the file tab was followed by the letter "T", and making the connection with Empendwe.

Paxton's voice was hoarse. "When does he normally get in?"

The Mining Engineer looked at his watch. It was ten past seven. "Eight, eight thirty."

"Can I have his address, please?"

While they studied the file, Thacker was brought to an interrogation room in the basement, unshaven and half-dressed, and was told to sit at the table facing the door. Shortly after ten, he looked up as the door opened and Paxton came into the room.

At that moment, the officious protestations which Thacker had been rehearsing for over two hours unravelled. He saw Paxton's bloodshot eyes, recognized his file, and a knife seemed to slice through his internal organs. His heart began to pound, he became short of breath, and his mind dissolved into inarticulate, fragmented thoughts.

Without taking his eyes off the man, Paxton sat across the table, laying the file down carefully in front of him. "We are examining your bank accounts," he said calmly. "I just want to know what you have been promised as a final payment."

Thacker tried to pull himself together. With an immense effort, he found his voice, which emerged louder than usual. "I know nothing about any payments. I wish to consult a…"

Before he had finished speaking, Paxton had stepped around the table, which was bolted to the floor. Gripping Thacker's open shirt collar on both sides and squeezing his clenched fists together under the man's chin, he lifted him out of his chair and slammed him violently against the wall. Then he turned, picked up Thacker's chair and gestured towards it. "Shall we continue?" he asked in an eerily calm tone of voice.

Thacker staggered to his feet and backed against the wall, panic in his eyes and in his stomach. He sensed that Paxton was ready to snap like a hair-trigger, that he would kill instantaneously and without a flicker of compassion. He also sensed that to dispose of a body would not be a problem in this building. Slowly, drawn by Paxton's icy stare, he crept back to the table and sat down.

"We have compared the drawings you produced at the mine with the survey at the time the mine last changed hands," Paxton continued. "We can see how you traced and altered the originals."

"By deliberately falsifying the records and misleading the mine operators, you are responsible for the death of a hundred or more miners." Paxton spoke in a monotone, his voice dull with exhaustion. "Now I will give you a choice. You can be charged with manslaughter, and you can then pay a lawyer to defend you and appeal your conviction. Because you *will* be convicted. The public will demand blood for this. You will spend your savings, you will mortgage your house, and you will still spend the rest of your life in prison."

"Or you can tell me what I need to know. You will remain in custody until the information has been verified, and if it turns out to be correct you will then be charged with a lesser offence."

Thacker needed no further persuasion. Three hours later, he was taken to a holding cell, and Paxton left the building to return to the hospital.

By mid afternoon, back in his office, he had reached Wim in Toronto. "I'll be there early next week," he said after breaking the news. "The funeral will be tomorrow. Then I'll be with Arnold in the U.K."

His mind reeling, Wim asked, "Can I come back for the funeral?"

"No. You're still on the 'wanted' list." Paxton spoke tersely. The funeral would be private, like his grief. Nothing could be allowed to distract him from what had to be done now.

42

Like Paxton, Wim and Stefan suffered an agony of love, shock and remorse at Selya's death. Both felt they might have done something to avert the disaster, and tortured themselves with thoughts of what might have been. Being on the other side of the world, unable to pay their last respects, added to their pain.

The next day, Chamberlain called Stefan to his office. "I'm sorry to tell you that there's been an accident at your mine," he announced. "Quite a large claim, in fact. The mine is probably a total loss."

Stefan was careful not to indicate that he had already heard about the disaster. "I just wanted you to know," Chamberlain continued quickly, "that we're handling it. In fact, because of the size, I've taken over the file personally, although the system shows Gavin as the handler. He'll be helping with the routine aspects."

Stefan nodded. He found it curious that Grince would be involved in the claim, since the policy had been written in the General Division.

"I think you would agree that if anyone says anything to you about it, it would be best if you say you know nothing about it, and leave it at that," Chamberlain said. "It might complicate matters if people found out that you were involved with the mine—and with the report which may have led the authorities to allow the mine to continue operating," he added pointedly, watching Stefan's reaction closely.

Stefan summoned all his will-power to keep his face expressionless. "My report actually drew attention to a potentially dangerous condition," he replied in a level tone.

But having opened the can of worms, Chamberlain was dismissing the topic with a wave of his hand. "People say different things," he said. "But that's why it would be best if you keep a low profile. Trust me. I've been in this business a long time." He gave Stefan a conspiratorial smile.

"By the way," Chamberlain continued, "I'd appreciate your helping Marlene to get involved in the large losses—you remember I asked you to help her. She hasn't had much exposure to anything complex."

Stefan was puzzled. Weeks ago, he had given Clewer summaries of his most contentious cases, inviting her to discuss them further or to attend meetings with the investigators, experts and other players whenever she wished, but Clewer had yet to respond. He had also asked her to review an account from legal counsel in the Poxidyl case, but again, several weeks had elapsed in silence. In contrast, Stefan was struck by the fact that he and his colleagues had to slave on a relentless conveyor belt of both routine and unexpected problems and tasks, all of which had to be dealt with immediately.

"Actually, I have offered to..." he began. But Chamberlain was standing, to signal an end to the meeting.

Stefan needed time to think. The news that Turr had bribed Thacker had come as a shock, but the insinuation that his report could be used to mitigate Thacker's guilt was unbearable.

That evening, he spoke to Wim about Chamberlain's remarks. Wim listened closely, then said, "Stefan, you were set up, mate. Turr must have doctored your report. You knew something which could have scuttled his project, so he found a way to isolate you, but at the same time use you to get the operation approved."

"He must have destroyed my original report," Stefan muttered.

"Don't worry, we'll take care of the bastard."

While they waited for Paxton, Stefan continued to work at Imperial Platinum. Every day he would find a pile of files on his desk, each with a note in Grince's back-slanted little capitals stapled to it. The pile would be set directly in front of his chair, as if to imply that the notes were certain to be more important, and worthy of immediate attention, than any other work he was doing. But the notes would invariably refer to a minor clerical procedure, or raise redundant questions about the policy wording or about the way the case was proceeding. Stefan had no time to ponder Grince's motives, but the time he had to spend in responding to the notes added to the flood of paperwork, and to his irritation.

At the same time, he became used to seeing Clewer's buxom profile plodding past his cubicle on the way to Grince's office. Clewer never came to see Stefan, however, nor did she respond to his invitations to discuss or take part in any of his claims.

The day after his meeting with Chamberlain, a reinsurance company representative called to ask Stefan about the Empendwe claim. Heeding Chamberlain's advice, Stefan told the man that he was not involved in the claim, but in answer to a general question, expressed the opinion that engineers and accountants should be among the team of investigators looking into such a claim.

After his new computer terminal had been installed, Stefan had found that he could no longer read work which he had transcribed on to diskettes at home. After experimenting a few times, he asked a secretary one day whether she could help.

The secretary called the young woman who had installed his new terminal, and after some discussion, they told Stefan that the system was now too advanced to be able to read his work.

"I'm sorry to hear that," he said. "We are typing most of our letters and reports ourselves, and I find I can do some of it at home in the evenings. It has been quite convenient to bring a diskette into the office the next day, and print it here, since the printers here are better than mine."

"You will have to upgrade your computer," said the young woman.

"That gives me an idea," Stefan said. "I could simply buy a new printer." Then another thought came to him. "Perhaps the company has some used printers for sale." He had seen a bulletin recently advertising old office furniture and equipment to be sold on the premises.

"Call Mary Oakes. She can tell you about that."

Mary told him that there were in fact printers available. They were due to be replaced the following week. However, they were leased printers. The lease had expired, and if anyone wished to buy one, the price was set by the contract.

Stefan gasped when he heard the price. "I think I could buy a new one for that price," he said. Mary agreed.

Within the hour, Grince asked to see Stefan in his office. He followed dutifully.

When he entered Grince's office, he found Clewer sitting at the table. "Close the door," she said.

Stefan detected a peremptory note in her voice, but said nothing. He closed the door. Grince sat down heavily, setting his face in a stony expression.

Grince and Clewer stared at Stefan from opposite angles, so that he felt he was under the spotlight at an inquisition. He waited stoically, enduring the insult of the stage-management, unable to imagine what could possibly be the reason for it.

"You have attempted to have your home equipped with office equipment, contrary to the company guidelines," Clewer bleated, as if delivering a verdict.

Stefan was so flabbergasted that for a moment he was speechless. Then he said hoarsely, "Would you explain, please?"

"It has come to our attention," Grince said, "that you have attempted to procure company equipment for home use, without going through the proper channels."

Stefan had now had enough. By typing his own work, and by using his own equipment on his own time, he had gone beyond the call of duty. But far from giving due credit, he saw that Grince and Clewer were bent on fabricating petty and insulting charges. Disgust and revulsion welled up inside him.

With an effort, he steadied himself, caught his breath and recounted the facts. Neither Grince nor Clewer moved, their faces like masks. Eventually, Clewer snapped, "Forget that."

"I'm sorry," Stefan said, "but I don't think I can possibly forget this." He had regained his composure, but his sense of outrage was growing.

"We show our leadership by putting disagreements behind us and moving forward," Clewer bleated.

Stefan said nothing. Surely problems ought to be resolved *before* anyone moves forward, he thought. Otherwise, we build on an improper footing.

"This is how I want you to govern yourself, going forward," Clewer continued, thrusting a document at him. "You can sign this, or not, as you wish," she added.

Stefan realized that he had reached his limit, his line in the sand. The woman had staged this confrontation without having the courtesy to speak to him first to check her facts. He wondered whether she saw herself as immune from censure or retaliation, just as a lawyer who spews out unsupported and defamatory allegations in a statement of claim is protected by statutory immunity against libel proceedings. Perhaps that was why she felt no need to check her facts—if one missile missed its mark, another could be launched with impunity, against a target which she felt was unable to counter-attack.

Perhaps it was also part of her training, Stefan thought, to be less concerned with facts than with plausible effect. If it won over a judge or jury, a convincing performance was more valuable than the truth. Stefan wondered whether this was what Frank Gallagher meant by "smoke and mirrors".

But whatever her motives, Stefan thought, it was unforgivable to use these tactics against a fellow-employee. While paying lip-service to the culture of equality and team-spirit touted by the president, she had adopted the tone of a magistrate lording it over a miscreant. Instead of apologising for the unwarranted accusation, she had maintained a hostile posture, and was now, in addition, presuming to dictate terms to him, as if to a servant.

"I'm not sure I should read this," he said calmly, hiding his outrage.

Clewer's face turned white. While she had not expected Stefan to be a willing victim, she had expected him to swallow his resentment and to react with the automatic deference and acquiescence she was used to seeing in office workers. Suddenly, she felt personally threatened, and found herself driven to dispose of this man, this male, with a new sense of urgency.

"Now I think you would agree that we have to act as a team," Grince said pretentiously.

"I think we have already discussed that. Every day I work as a member of a team, perhaps more than most people," Stefan replied.

"And we have to act professionally," Grince added.

Stefan said nothing. He found the remark insulting, but he would not dignify Grince by asking his advice on the meaning of the word "professional".

Grince continued, "It was also unfortunate that you saw fit to make comments on the African mine claim to Harold Bell at First Reinsurance."

Stefan shook his head. "I answered a general question," he replied, feeling that he was now the target of missiles flying randomly at him from different directions.

"You answered a general question?" Grince echoed sarcastically. "As I understand it, the advice given by you would apply specifically to this claim, and we have now had to respond to demands from our reinsurers for a full scale investigation."

"This would normally be required," Stefan answered.

"This would normally be required?" Grince sneered. "Strange as it may seem to you, we don't deal in generalities. This happens to be a valued account, through a valued broker." He looked at Stefan as though expecting him to realize that he had overlooked a hallowed rule of insurance equity.

When Stefan did not answer, Grince continued, "Fortunately, we were able to reach a lawyer with a pragmatic approach, who understood the importance of the account. He was able to impress on the reinsurers when we met with them yesterday that there would be nothing to gain from an exhaustive investigation, and an important account to lose if any controversy developed. Mr. Chamberlain is concerned that there be no controversy, let alone litigation, on this account, and the insured would certainly sue if we resisted the claim in any way. We were able to settle for policy limits of a hundred million, to avoid the cost of litigation which you almost succeeded in precipitating." He smirked, pleased with his turn of phrase.

"It was obvious that the loss exceeded policy limits," Grince added, "and that the limits were payable even after applying the fifty-thousand deductible to the loss. But it would have been necessary to waive the deductible in any event, in view of your interference, in order to preserve the insured's good-will towards the company. Yep."

Again hiding his outrage, Stefan listened with a thoughtful expression which Grince took to be a sign of acquiescence. In fact, Stefan was pondering Grince's motives in expediting Turr's claim. A veneration for the "valued broker" and the "valued account" was certainly a driving force in insurance ethics, and a large international account, backed by a large brokerage, automatically commanded preferential treatment. Also, Chamberlain was apparently anxious to accommodate Turr, and as a member of the hierarchy, Chamberlain was to be obeyed without question. These two facts of insurance life apart, Stefan had also noticed that Grince liked to play the man of high finance, impressing employees of other companies with his cool indifference when millions were in play. The fact that reinsurers would be paying ninety-five per cent of the claim would have added to Grince's motivation, Stefan thought; and the chance to ascribe blame to a fellow-employee, however specious the criticism, would be an important bonus.

"On the other hand," Grince continued while these thoughts were turning over in Stefan's mind, "a payment was apparently authorized by you today which was improper from a coverage point of view."

"Which claim is this?" Stefan asked, puzzled.

"The claim of Helga Wilkinson." Grince stared at him, waiting for a flicker of recognition which he hoped would also contain a hint of fear and guilt.

Stefan recalled the claim. The insured, an old lady, had been surrounded by a mob of teen-aged girls at the Eaton Centre, a large downtown mall in Toronto, and had been robbed of her purse, her watch and jewellery, and a dress which she had just bought for her granddaughter's birthday. Stefan had taken a call from her broker, who represented a small, storefront insurance office in a suburban strip-mall. The broker had complained that six months had passed since the robbery, but that that his client had still not been paid.

Stefan had found the claim on his computer and had spoken to the handler, who told him that Mrs. Wilkinson had not yet "replaced" some of the stolen items. The amount she would have to pay if she were to replace them would then be "depreciated" if she wished to settle her claim now. If she were to replace any of the items later, the company would then consider paying the balance. "I'm waiting for Mrs. Wilkinson to advise how she wishes to proceed," the handler told Stefan.

"Mrs. Wilkinson has been insured with Imperial Platinum—or the Platinum, as it was, and before that, the old Venus Assurance, for thirty-five years," the broker told Stefan, "and this is her first claim. She has replaced as many of the items as she can afford, but she can't understand why there has to be a fifteen-percent deduction for depreciation on the other items. Either her calls are not returned, or she gets a different person every time, and she's getting nowhere."

The handler told Stefan that when an item had not been replaced, the company's standard practice was to deduct fifteen percent, which happened to be the total of the sales taxes which a retailer added to the amount shown on the price tag. Stefan pointed out that the amount of the tax was irrelevant to the amount of depreciation: if the item lost were new, like the dress Mrs. Wilkinson had bought for her granddaughter, it would not have depreciated at all, while something old might have lost most of its value. In Mrs. Wilkinson's case, Stefan felt that the dress, the jewellery and the watch were worth as much at the time of the robbery as when she had acquired them, so that no deduction for depreciation should be applied. He also felt that Mrs. Wilkinson had waited long enough, and he had recommended payment of the full amount of the replacement cost, including the tax.

"Of course, the policy deductible was taken into account," Stefan told Grince after he had explained the matter.

"The policy deductible was taken into account?" Grince echoed sarcastically. "But you would have preferred to waive that as well, when you were being so generous with the company's money? Has it occurred to you that unless a purchase is made, no money is payable at all, and the tax is therefore not payable under the policy?"

"You could just as well say that unless a purchase is made, no money is payable at all," Stefan replied, "so that the policy should pay nothing. But the policy does provide that something is payable when an item has not been replaced. We pay the amount it would cost to replace the item—which includes the tax—less depreciation or betterment, if any." He considered adding that Mrs. Wilkinson's claim, apart from the stolen cash, amounted to little more than five hundred dollars: even if fifteen per cent were to be deducted, Grince was quibbling about the grand sum of seventy-five dollars.

Grince made a snorting sound. "There were items...perfume, hand cream and so on in the purse," he said, "which were not replaced with due diligence and dispatch, as required by the policy. Proper depreciation should have been taken by you on these and the other items. In the circumstances, I have countermanded your authorization, and the claim will be properly adjusted according to policy requirements. Yep."

There was a long pause. Stefan had the impression that Grince and Clewer expected him to say something else, but he felt too insulted and degraded to continue the conversation.

Eventually, Grince dismissed him with an ominous "Well, we'll have to consider our options. Thank you," he added loudly and ungraciously, as if to prevent Stefan from saying anything further.

As Stefan was closing the door, he glanced back into the office and saw Clewer rolling her eyes at Grince. As he walked away from the office, he heard Grince's falsetto giggle behind the closed door.

*   *   *

When Mrs. Wilkinson received her cheque three weeks later, she saw that twenty-three dollars and fifteen cents had been deducted, without explanation, in addition to the policy deductible of two hundred and fifty dollars. After exchanging messages with Grince for two days, her broker was treated to a lecture about the application of measures of depreciation, when items have not been replaced with the requisite due diligence and dispatch. "You would do well to refer Mrs. Wilkinson to the relevant provisions," Grince told the broker in a tone which implied that his patience, abundant though it was, had its limits.

A few months later, when Mrs. Wilkinson's policy was renewed for another year, she noticed that the premium had increased. Called into service again, the broker spoke with the underwriter.

"We don't normally forgive burglary and theft claims," the underwriter told him, referring to her manual.

"Mrs. Wilkinson was robbed on a downtown street in broad daylight." The broker fought to control his exasperation. "If her house had been burgled, there might be some reason to question how secure the premises were, or to consider whether the crime rate in her area justified an increase, but in this case she was a totally innocent victim."

But it was only after the broker had pleaded with supervisors, managers and Head Office executives, finally threatening to have his client complain to the Superintendent of Insurance, that Imperial Platinum, citing "public relations", cancelled Mrs. Wilkinson's increase in premium.

"These f-g brokers," Barbara Fleam growled, to obsequious titters from her retinue.

At the end of the year, the broker's contract, which entitled him to arrange insurance for his clients through Imperial Platinum, was not renewed.

43

Paxton came straight to the point. "The armed forces will be delivering humanitarian supplies to Grenada and the Dominican Republic next week," he said, "and one of their aircraft has room for the three of us." He stopped abruptly, as if briefing his troops, giving them time to digest the information before proceeding.

Wim and Stefan were listening closely. Paxton continued, "The route will be due south to the Gulf of Mexico, then east. The Caymans are on the flight path, or close. We will be dropped off on Grand Cayman."

They were in Paxton's hotel room, overlooking Nathan Phillips Square and the City Hall. A clock across the square, sounding like London's Big Ben, struck the half hour. Stefan glanced at his watch. It was ten thirty in the evening. "I think we have more privacy when we use military aircraft," he said.

"There are a few advantages," Paxton agreed. "Civilian airlines prohibit firearms, for one."

"Did you manage to bring a gun?" Wim asked.

"No. But I have contacts here."

"Does anyone back home know what you're doing?"

"Polo knows. I haven't talked to many people." His expression darkened.

"Do we know that our friend will be at home when we get there?" Wim asked.

"We know he has a flight booked to Sao Paulo next Wednesday, which means he'll still be on his island on Tuesday night. That's the night we pay him a visit."

"Did you know that the mine is insured by a company here in Toronto?" Stefan asked him.

"I saw that in Thacker's file, yes." He paused. "But whether the mine was sabotaged for insurance money, or whether it was a case of blatant disregard for the workers' safety, the result was the same, and the man has to pay."

Stefan told him that he was working at the insurance company, at Turr's behest. He also recounted his conversation with Chamberlain about the Empendwe claim.

"So Turr has a man in the insurance company," Paxton said. "That adds another wrinkle." He was silent for a while before turning to Stefan. "I was planning to take you with us, since you know the layout of Turr's place. In fact, I faxed the base today to confirm our names. But now I think you should stay here. Continue to turn up at work, so that nothing appears out of the ordinary. Just keep a low profile—and don't try to blow the whistle on the claim. You'd probably be outranked, but most importantly, this Chamberlain could realize that someone has talked. I don't want Turr to get any warning."

Stefan nodded.

"These are papers I found on the mine manager's desk," Paxton continued, handing Wim a folder. "I'd like you both to look through them."

Wim picked up the folder and glanced at the contents. "We can go through it tonight," he said, "and report back to you tomorrow."

"You mentioned the mine manager," Wim asked Paxton. "Did you see him?"

"He apparently had a heart attack at the scene, and died on the way to hospital."

Wim and Stefan both flinched. They had known Martin as a good friend, one of the gang who had gone out to reopen Empendwe. The shock left them feeling physically assaulted.

"So Turr is responsible for two of our close friends, and a hundred others," Wim said after a long silence. "And if we don't take care of him, he'll carry on as if nothing has happened."

"That's essentially true," said Paxton. "He isn't even listed as an officer of ReExploration. Legally, he had nothing to do with the operation of the mine."

"And he could afford to tie up the courts for years anyway," Wim said. "Or until he had bought enough witnesses and experts."

"Of course there will be a commission of enquiry," Paxton said. "But it will drag on, and in the end all you will get is some criticism of procedures and a few recommendations. The commission will have no teeth, especially as far as Turr is concerned."

*   *   *

They met again late the next evening at Paxton's hotel. His face drawn, Wim put the package on the table.

"It was deliberate," he said.

Paxton's face was inscrutable.

Wim took a drawing from the envelope and unfolded it. "This is a map of the mine in cross-section," he told Paxton.

Stefan recognized the drawing. Much of it was in his own hand, but he could see that Selya had added details and extensions after he had left.

"Selya had been identifying flaws in the rock formation at various levels, based on seismological evidence and ore-body analysis," Wim continued. "She had been mapping the development at fifteen-hundred feet, over here—and the day before the collapse, she gave Martin the updated map with this memo." He reached into the package.

"Fifteen-hundred was never considered for development when I was at the mine," Stefan said.

"Nor when I was there," Wim said. "This was a case of high-grading, to spike productivity levels after the yield started to fall off. But it meant mining into the pillar. In the memo, Selya says she warned Martin against it a few days earlier. She then began mapping the area, and came up with some specific recommendations."

"She tells Martin in the memo that if any mining is carried out, against her recommendations, no blasting should take place in the areas specifically marked—here and here—because of geological flaws. These flaws, according to her calculations, would destabilize the shaft, causing rock-bursts higher up, but more than that, they would open fissures right up to the surface."

"Which would create a new route for the tailings to flood the mine," Stefan said.

"Exactly. Now Martin seems to have taken the warning seriously. Here is his fax to Turr the same day, attaching a copy of Selya's memo. But apparently Turr spoke to him on the phone—here's a hand-written note at the bottom of the page—and told him to blast as originally instructed—which was exactly where Selya had said not to blast."

"What reason was given?" Paxton asked.

"Martin doesn't say. Of course Turr could deny it, or say that Martin had misunderstood."

"But Turr had to know himself what was going to happen," Paxton said.

"Absolutely. Selya spelled it out clearly, and Turr himself is a geologist."

"But surely Martin would make sure the mine was evacuated before the blasting took place?"

"The mine *was* evacuated. Martin must have thought it was safe to send the crews back in after two or three hours."

"He miscalculated, then."

"Martin was a good man, but he needed more experience. Of course that's probably why Turr put him in charge. He could be easily manipulated."

"But Turr should have told him to keep the workers out…"

"At least six hours in this case. Probably longer. But obviously he never gave the workers a thought."

"And Selya herself—why would she have gone back so soon?"

"She would never have expected Martin to blast exactly where she had told him not to blast. Nobody would expect that."

"But as we can see, Martin took his orders from Turr," Paxton said. "So as I thought, it's Turr we have to deal with."

44

They reached the base after a two hour drive the following Tuesday evening, and were directed to an administrative building half a mile inside the gates. Paxton introduced himself to the duty officer. "We have an appointment with…"—he took a folded sheet of paper out of his pocket, then to Stefan's surprise read out the name, "Corporal A. Peters."

Annette arrived five minutes later. Careful not to show that she recognized Stefan, she greeted them politely and led them outside to her jeep. She was dressed in fatigues, and wearing a beret.

Sensing that she preferred to appear impersonal, Stefan took his leave and returned to the car. On the pretext of giving him directions, Annette came over and leaned into the car. "I didn't realize you weren't going," she whispered. "This took some arranging," she added with a wry smile.

Trying to understand what she meant, Stefan said, "It was a last-minute decision, but I think they can take care of it without me."

She wanted to say more, to spend time with him. She had gone out of her way to be on this flight after intercepting Paxton's message.

He said quickly, "They'll be back in two or three days. I'll be in touch." Impulsively, he put his hand over hers, and looked into her eyes. It was a moment neither of them wanted to end.

She drove Wim and Paxton to the airstrip, where a Hercules transport was waiting. They began to thank her, but she followed them up the steps. "I'm going with you," she said. "I'm navigating."

<h1 style="text-align:center">45</h1>

Fleam was standing in her office as Clewer entered. Her flushed face told Clewer that the news was good.

"Jenner has made me the new president for Canada. I'll be reporting to him of course," she added breathlessly. "And you are succeeding Clive."

Clewer whooped with joy, and they embraced, laughing and moaning.

Fleam explained that Jenner had been promoted to World Headquarters, and had appointed her to take over in Toronto. Then she told Clewer that Chamberlain had made an unexpected decision to retire, apparently unconnected with Jenner's departure.

"Now," Fleam continued. "To get you off on the right foot with your team, you need to do something decisive, and we've talked about Kristiansson a couple of times. Any progress?"

Clewer told Fleam about the recent meeting with Stefan in Grince's office.

"Perfect," Fleam said. "Now you can say he acted beyond his authority, and refused to co-operate with your plan to move forward."

"Well, he actually had a persuasive explanation. Of course, I didn't admit..."

"Let me tell you something. This isn't a court of law, thank God. We went over this. You make the accusation, and if he rolls over and turns the other cheek, it's as good as a confession. If he argues, you have him for not being co-operative, not being a team player, and you still make the accusation. You have him both ways. It's a win-win situation. All we have to do now is fire him, citing 'recent events', without specifying what they were, and saying 'we have no alternative'. Put a memo in his personnel file referring to the computer, and mention his refusal to read your directives. Unco-operative, not a team player, not in sync with the Three Principles. Whatever. You'll see how easy it is. With a flick of the finger, he'll be gone. Out in the street, like the winos on the grates out there."

"Of course, if he sues..."

"It doesn't matter. He's gone anyway. If he sues, it's handled by Spinks, Spinks and Rutter. But they don't sue. Or if they do, they drop the suit after a couple of years, because it's costing more in lawyers' fees than they would get. And it's costing them in frustration and loss of sleep, because we can stall indefinitely. We use Spinks because he can stonewall until the cows come home—and the longer he drags it out, the longer their own lawyer's meter runs, at two-hundred-and-fifty an hour or whatever. It's the same leverage we have against people with claims, especially the ones who don't have the money to keep on paying their lawyers."

Fleam paused to take a breath, then continued, "We can also get fellow employees to testify against them—they know which side their bread's buttered on. They don't need much persuasion to start bad-mouthing their ex-colleagues anyway. And we can keep digging up little things..."

"Gavin's good at that. Anything petty and bureaucratic—that's what he lives for..."

"Don't worry, his turn will come. But right now, we have to take care of Kristiansson. This is how you start making a name for yourself. You'll see how docile and compliant the rest get when you liquidate one of them. That's how you consolidate your position. If it means siding with Grince for a while…"

"Gavin keeps harping about the professional liability files. Of course it's one of his myopic hangups—or maybe it's a game he's playing—but as you say, we can support him for the time being…"

"And remember to say 'We' when you write the termination letter. It implies that the whole company is making the decision, rather than one or two people. But the Personnel Department will have a sample letter. See Pinker about it. Mention my name. There'll be some loose ends—notice period and so on. They know about those things—they had plenty of practice when I was cleansing my departments. In fact, they'll probably have a standard letter on file."

*   *   *

Grince busily scraped his soup bowl, tilting it towards him, then flicked imaginary crumbs from his lap and scoured his hands to complete the ritual. He blinked with a pained expression, as if to appear preoccupied with thought, then began to claw at a piece of blue cornflour and walnut bread. The restaurant, one of many offering sophisticated cuisine to beneficiaries of expense accounts, was crowded and noisy.

Across the table, Clewer waited until Grince had stopped fidgetting. Then, looking into his eyes, pitching her thin voice as low as possible, she said, "There's something I have to tell you."

Grince suffered a pang of apprehension, sensing that he was about to hear of a shift of power within the hierarchy. He was disturbed by the thought that Clewer might have a direct line to a higher level.

"Clive Chamberlain is retiring," Clewer continued, waiting for him to digest the information.

"I thought he had two more years." Grince affected mild, detached surprise, relieved to have time to prepare himself to hear who would succeed Chamberlain.

"Well, he apparently decided a few months ago that he would retire this year, without telling anyone. Then he had this large claim to handle, the Zambia mine, and he decided it would be his last hurrah."

Grince giggled. "He has one claim to handle, and it finishes him," he joked, anxious to appear unconcerned about the succession.

Clewer gave him half a smile and waited. Then she said, "I'm to be V.-P. General Division."

Grince felt his stomach drop, but he was glad to have prepared himself. His face still creased by the insincere giggle, he was able to hide his shock and disappointment. "Congratulations," he forced himself to say.

"Now to more important things," Clewer continued briskly, to imply that she was above the vanities of title and politics. "You and I are both committed to the Three Principles, which gives us common ground to work from."

Grince nodded, grateful to be considered loyal to the Principles.

"With Jenner moving to New York, we have a new order to establish, under Barbara."

Grince's stomach plummetted again. This was another blow. His face tightened, and this time he could find nothing to say. His throat dried up, and he struggled to swallow.

"Moving forward, and working together," Clewer continued, "I think we need to look at our team. There are one or two dinosaurs around, of course, but they may still have their contributions to make." she said dismissively. "Then there are people who have been close to Clive and the old order. Will they fit in now? This is what we have to think about." She waited for his reaction.

Grince thought quickly. The sensitive information he had compiled on people like Chamberlain had helped him to survive reorganizations in the past. But he had not expected Chamberlain to leave so soon, and he had no leverage against Fleam or Clewer. He would have to accept their terms.

In truth, he had no choice in any event. From his earliest days as the curly-haired teacher's pet, holding her hand in the school yard, ingratiating himself by informing against classmates, and then as the government clerk, piously following arbitrary rules and regulations both for their own sake and as a means to gain ascendancy over others, his course had been set. The institution, with its bureaucracy and its hierarchy, was his life and his creed. Of course he would genuflect before his new mistresses.

But as the president had said, change could be made to work to one's advantage. He would embrace change, and he would move forward with the new order, using it as far as possible to continue pursuing his own agenda.

Seizing the opportunity, he said, "Kristiansson hasn't exactly shown himself to be a team player. On the contrary, he seems to have preferred to report to Clive rather than to me, and certainly nothing I have said seems to have been acknowledged or acted upon by him. As you may know, I keep detailed notes on all my staff, and I'll be happy to provide them to you. Essentially, if we're reviewing membership in our team, I'd have to recommend that we discontinue his membership."

Clewer sipped her coffee and looked at Grince. "Leave it to me," she said.

*   *   *

Chamberlain left the company in a flurry of receptions and farewells, the last of which took place in a large ground-floor training room which doubled as a venue for celebrations of various kinds. Passers-by on the street outside, either at mid-day or in mid-afternoon, were apt to see clusters of people profiled at the windows, wine glasses in hand. Stefan had attended receptions there for people who had logged twenty years with the company in one case, and twenty-five in another, and he had toasted Chamberlain himself only a few months earlier at his sixtieth-birthday celebration.

When a senior employee was the guest of honour, the gatherings would be graced by the appearance of an executive, and so it was on this occasion. In a crimson outfit which attracted attention and repelled at the same time, Barbara Fleam was surrounded by people who felt sufficiently elevated in the hierarchy to approach the heir apparent, and who needed to feel close to the inner circle, if only at a social event. Conscious of an invisible barrier, the others kept their distance, congregating according to their stripe, underwriters with underwriters, in-house-lawyers with in-house-lawyers, S.I.U. people with S.I.U. people, clerical people with clerical people, adjusters with adjusters.

"Now you see how a level playing-field works, corporate-style," Frank Cameron said to Stefan through the side of his mouth as they refilled their plastic wine-glasses.

Stefan laughed. "It might help to level the field if we started a sports team."

"Do you see anybody who would qualify?" Frank smiled. "What did you have in mind?"

"Well, they play ice-hockey here, and in Sweden too. I played it as a boy."

"Hockey…I don't know. You need something more multi-cultural in Toronto now."

"Well, there is no game more multi-cultural than cricket. It's played in more countries throughout the world than any other game—throughout the Carribbean, Australia, New Zealand, Africa, India, Pakistan, Sri Lanka, England…"

"I heard there are over a hundred teams here in Toronto, believe it or not. But you must have noticed, the 'mainstream' attitude is still quite condescending towards cricket. And you have to admit, the rules are hard to understand."

"No more than baseball. Actually, I find baseball more difficult…"

While Stefan and Frank were arguing the relative merits of baseball and cricket, Fleam and her retinue had moved to another window. Glancing outside, she caught sight of two homeless men, grizzled and unkempt, on the sidewalk grate beside the building. She could also see their sleeping bags, discarded coffee cups, and an empty wine bottle.

"…with a ninety-eight per cent operating ratio across the book of business, we can expect a net profit again this year over the hundred million mark…" she was declaiming, her audience hanging on every word, assuming grave, responsible expressions.

"…is there nothing we can do about those hobos?" she snarled at a man on her right, interrupting herself.

"The police can't seem to spare the manpower," the man replied. "When we call them, they…"

"…Then hire more security. They're on private property."

The man kept his voice as mild and tentative as possible. "Actually, they're on city…" he began.

Fleam bridled at the contradiction. "…Go and speak to Don Gibson over there," she barked. "He probably has contacts who would take care of it. Tell him to come and see me later."

Just then, one of the homeless men looked up at the window. Catching sight of Fleam, he raised an imaginary glass in salute.

Flushed with indignation, Fleam left the room to return to the executive wing.

Clewer moved into Chamberlain's office the following day. Neither she nor Grince discussed her new role with Stefan, and he continued to work at his desk, assuming that he would report to Clewer as he had to Chamberlain.

Early in the afternoon, a secretary came to tell him that Clewer wished to see him at two o'clock. He thought it unusual to receive such a summons through a third party, when Clewer might have called him directly, but gave the matter no further thought.

At five minutes to two, the secretary returned to remind him of the appointment. He continued to work until two, then went up to Clewer's new office.

When he entered, Clewer was behind the desk, but to Stefan's surprise, Don Gibson was seated in front of the desk, on the right hand side. Stefan greeted them affably.

Gibson was wearing an expression which Stefan had never seen before, a ghastly grimace of embarrassment or discomfort.

"What is going on?" Stefan asked him.

"I was just asked to sit in on this," Gibson answered. He seemed anxious to convey that he had had no prior involvement in whatever was to be discussed.

Puzzled, Stefan saw Clewer close the door, then head back to her chair. She began to read from a paper on the desk in front of her. Out of the corner of his eye, Stefan saw Gibson, his eyes fixed in an unblinking stare, shift into a crouching position on the edge of his chair.

"Due to recent events," she read, "we have no alternative but to terminate your employment. The terms are as foll…"

But Stefan was already out of the office, on his way to the elevator, his only thought to get into the open air.

46

They landed on Grand Cayman shortly after three in the morning. Wim and Paxton thanked Annette and the crew. "We'll be back before you take off," Paxton told them. They had until noon.

A military van drew up as they got out of the plane. The driver said a few words to Paxton, then got out and led them to the back of the van. They climbed inside, and the driver closed the doors.

After a short drive, the van stopped. The driver came to let them out, and they found themselves on a gravelled area overlooking a boat harbour. Paxton quietly thanked the driver, and the van groaned off into the night.

"This way," Paxton said in a low voice, walking quickly on to a timber walkway. Passing the boats moored to the dock without a glance, he headed towards the end of the dock, then turned abruptly on to a jetty and stopped at the third boat on his right. In the clear moonlight, Wim made out the name, "*Nightjar II*".

Wim followed Paxton aboard, and they checked below to be sure they were alone. Then he untied the moorings as Paxton started the engine and manoeuvred the boat out of its berth.

When they had cleared the harbour, Paxton took a chart out of his pocket. "This is the route," he said, opening the throttle.

Wim spread the chart on the table below. He noted the Caymans, and off to the east, a small, unnamed island. The route Paxton had charted would take them north of the island about five miles.

Paxton set his course and came below. "We'll be there within the hour," he told Wim. He looked around, then lifted one of the bench seats and pulled out a sports bag. "This is some gear we may need," he said as he unzipped it. Wim saw a coil of rope, which he estimated at two hundred feet, a crowbar, steel hooks and claws, studded boots and a pick axe.

Paxton took a revolver out of a holster on his waist and slid it over the table towards Wim. "I'll take this man with my bare hands," he said. "Just be ready to cover me if anybody else shows up."

They came in quietly towards the north side of the island. Paxton cut the engine a hundred yards offshore, and they drifted in, weighing anchor twenty yards from land. Wim had inflated a dingy, which they lowered into the water with the sports bag and paddles. They climbed down into the dingy, knowing they could swim back if necessary.

The island was as steep and densely wooded on the north side as the south, and to free both hands for the climb, Wim slung the bag over his shoulder. They climbed for the best part of an hour, until they reached the peak and began a gradual descent towards the south.

In the murky light of dawn, the chateau came into view through the trees at the edge of a steep ravine. Paxton gestured towards the bag, which Wim took off his shoulder and laid on the ground. He took out the coil of rope, tied one end around a branch and tested it with his weight.

Paxton took the crowbar and wedged it under his belt, rejecting the rest of the gear with a quick motion of his hand. He turned towards Wim, who began to slide down the slope, using trees to slow his descent.

The slope ended in a stone wall about fifteen feet high, where the hillside had been excavated to level the property, and the rope gave out just below the top of the wall. Wim found a toehold in the stones, grasped the top of the wall, then dropped quietly to the ground. Paxton, athletic despite his bulk, followed close behind.

They moved quickly across the gravel to the side of the house, then around to the front. Paxton brought out his skeleton keys and crouched against the door. Two minutes later, the lock opened.

Slowly, all his senses straining, he pushed the door ajar, then stood still, listening. The house was silent. He glanced back at Wim, who had the revolver in his hand, then carefully put one foot inside the doorway and put his weight on it. No floorboards creaked, and no alarm sounded.

They eased themselves over the threshold, and Wim gently closed the door. Despite Stefan's assurances, force of habit made Paxton scan the hallway for security cameras. But Stefan had been right. The island was naturally secure, and visitors arrived by helicopter, in full view. Turr would have seen no need to install security equipment.

Silently, they crossed the hallway and went upstairs, pausing again to listen for sounds of movement. It was five thirty, and the house was still as quiet as a tomb.

Having memorized a plan of the house which Stefan had sketched for him, Paxton moved quickly to Turr's office. Once again, he used his skeleton keys. Then, standing to the right of the door, he grasped the knob and slowly turned it. Wim stood on the other side, revolver in hand.

After a few seconds, Paxton slowly pushed the door open a few inches, noting a slight resistance as it grazed over carpeting on the floor. Carefully releasing the doorknob so as to make no sound, he stepped inside the office. Wim checked the hallway again, then followed, closing the door behind him as slowly and carefully as Paxton had opened it.

Apart from slivers of light beside heavy window curtains, Turr's office was in darkness. Paxton stepped behind the desk on his left to part the curtains a few inches, and they surveyed the room.

It was a long room, about twelve feet wide and thirty feet long, with curtained windows behind the desk and further along on their left side. There were curtained windows also at the other end of the room, facing the door they had passed through, and at that end of the room they could see leather sofas, a coffee table, a bookcase and another desk. An oriental rug was laid over the wall-to-wall carpeting near the sofas and the coffee table.

There was another door at the far corner of the room, on their right. Paxton motioned Wim to the window behind the desk, then crossed the room. Wim closed the curtains behind him, and as he did so, Paxton saw a light under the door.

The instant Paxton saw the light, it went out. He stepped quickly behind the door just as it inched open.

From the doorway, Turr could see nothing unusual. But something—a slight vibration, possibly a footfall—had sharpened his senses. He had turned on a light to check his bedroom and the ensuite leading from it, then turned off the light and stepped to the door.

He opened the door further, then called out Aaron's name. Still suspicious, he turned, intending to take a gun from his night table drawer.

But Paxton was already on him, locking his left arm around Turr's throat and smashing his right knee into his back. Turr staggered against what would normally have been a paralysing blow, then miraculously found his footing, spun round and speared his hands through Paxton's arm lock. With titanic strength, he broke Paxton's grip, grabbed his lapels and butted him full in the face.

But Paxton's hands were now behind Turr's neck, and without missing a beat, he pumped Turr's head down and brought his knee up into his face. Then, as Turr straightened up, Paxton sprang into the air, ramming Turr in the stomach with both feet.

The force of Paxton's two hundred and fifty pounds against his midriff sent even Turr's gigantic frame reeling. He staggered backwards, crashing into the wall behind him.

In a flash, Paxton had closed in on Turr, this time slamming his fist into the man's face with the force of a sledgehammer. Now Turr's knees began to buckle. He tried to straighten up, his huge hands weaving, his dark eyes fixed on Paxton.

But nothing could stop Paxton now. His fist crashed into Turr's face again, and again, until the man began to slide down the wall. Again Paxton rammed Turr in the chest with his feet, felling him to the floor. Then, with one foot on Turr's shoulder, and the other on his face, he kicked down hard, once, twice, until he heard the neck break.

Paxton turned away. The adrenalin-rush had dissipated, his legs and hands felt numb, and he felt drained. With a supreme effort, he squared his shoulders, tightened his abdominal muscles and strode through the doorway into the office. "One less scorpion," he said hoarsely.

Wim opened the door and checked the landing. The house was still quiet. Warily, they went down the stairs and crossed the hall to the entrance.

Without pausing in his stride, Paxton opened the door and stepped outside, followed by Wim. As he closed the door, Wim glanced into the house, and for an instant thought he saw a figure, perhaps that of a woman, moving quickly across the top of the stairs.

Revived by the fresh air, Paxton was ready for the return journey. They scaled the wall and pulled themselves up the ravine on the rope, which Wim untied and returned to the bag together with Paxton's crowbar. The going was easier in daylight, and they took the north slope at a canter, reaching the boat in less than an hour. After a short wait at the marina on Grand Cayman, they were picked up shortly after eleven and reunited with the crew of the Hercules. The excursion to Turr's island had taken just under eight hours.

*　　　　　*　　　　　*

Stefan drove out to meet them at the Canadian Forces base when they arrived two days later. Annette, who had three days' leave, agreed to come back with them to the city.

"She doesn't know," Wim told Stefan as they waited in the car for Annette.

"About Turr?"

"She knows about Empendwe. She doesn't know what happened to Turr."

On the highway, Annette turned to Stefan. "So how is your life as an insurance worker?" she asked.

Stefan told her of his experiences with Grince and Clewer, the false accusations, the termination.

Annette put her hand on his arm. "They did you a favour," she smiled. "You didn't want to have to tell your grandchildren you spent your life in insurance, did you?"

"On the other hand," Wim said, "you can't let them get away with it. That two-faced bitch, grabbing her chance to play prosecutor, judge and jury at your expense, then hiding behind an ex-cop. I'll bet he felt proud of himself. And that disgusting twerp. You know, mate, I've never thought this way before, but if there had just been a union..."

"I can sue, I suppose," Stefan said, thinking to himself that Wim was right. But so was Annette.

"But that doesn't settle the score," Wim replied. "The company pays something, but the individuals carry on scot-free. In fact, they'll now be puffing themselves up, giving themselves credit for being tough, or decisive, or some such crap. No, we have to take care of them, the same way we took care of the scorpions at Empendwe."

Stefan recalled Don Gibson's remark that he and his colleagues on the police force were never satisfied unless individual perpetrators, rather than corporate entities, had been made to pay. Then he had another thought. "Of course, the reinsurers could refuse to pay Imperial Platinum if they have evidence that the claim was fraudulent," he mused. "If they haven't paid already."

"Thacker's confession would certainly help to prove an element of fraud, at least," Wim said. "But five years from now, when the evidence has been manipulated this way and that, and they settle out of court on their lawyers' advice, the responsible parties will have retired or moved on, and it will simply be an accounting exercise to keep people like your friend Grince occupied."

"Chamberlain, the vice-president who authorized the payment to Turr, has retired already," Stefan said.

"Very likely with his cut. So they can all blame him. But that doesn't settle your score."

"Let it go," Annette told Stefan. "You can do something more worthwhile with your life."

Paxton, who had not said a word until now, spoke up. "It will be a pleasure," he said,looking towards Wim.

47

The compound and the cabins were deserted now, the vehicles and equipment were gone, and the hill called Empendwe had begun its healing process, digesting what remained of the human invasion which had tried to disembowel it. In fifty years, its surface wounds would have closed, and the grass once again would ripple in an unbroken expanse, host to the wildlife within it.

Across the globe, after merging and changing its name one more time, the Imperial Platinum would be swallowed by another corporate entity several times larger, which itself would then lay claim to noble lineage of over two hundred years. Every few years, a new era of teamwork, democracy and ethical service would be heralded by self-styled leaders; but behind the façade of the mantras and the propaganda, the Grinces and Clewers in their concrete stopes would continue to manipulate their mandate in a perennial quest for control, self-importance and security.

Free of such indulgences, the villagers on the banks of the Kafue would continue to hunt and fish, following the river as it rose and fell with the seasons. In time, they would forget the rape of Empendwe, but for the present, like the city beyond, the hill would be seen as a place to avoid, a canker on the face of nature, inhospitable to man and scorpion alike.